"Maybe you're too young to know how to handle men."

Bent lowered his voice. "Here's a tip for you. Don't come on so strong. Some will run off, be intimidated by a woman like you. But others—real men—will be challenged."

She swallowed and her heart seemed to have stopped beating.

"They'll chase till they catch you," he finished. "You'll be like a henhouse chick caught by a hungry wolf."

"I can take care of myself."

He looked skeptical.

She jerked her chin away and glared at him. Suddenly she was angry, too. "All your talk of challenges—why don't you rise to one, Bent? Stay and watch me ride tomorrow. If I don't have the talent, then go."

"No."

She stared at him. "You're scared, aren't you?" she whispered.

Dear Reader,

This month, Silhouette Romance has a wonderful lineup—sure to add love and laughter to your sunny summer days and sultry nights. Marie Ferrarella starts us off with another FABULOUS FATHER in *The Women in Joe Sullivan's Life*. Sexy Joe Sullivan was an expert on *grown* women, but when he suddenly finds himself raising three small nieces, he needs the help of Maggie McGuire—and finds himself falling for her womanly charms as well as her maternal instinct! Cassandra Cavannaugh has plans for her own BUNDLE OF JOY in Julianna Morris's *Baby Talk*. And Jake O'Connor had no intention of being part of them. Can true love turn Mr. Wrong into a perfect father—and husband for Cassie?

Dorsey Kelley spins another thrilling tale for WRANGLERS AND LACE in *Cowboy for Hire*. Bent Murray thought his rodeo days were behind him, until sassy cowgirl Kate Monahan forced him to face his past—and her place in his heart. Handsome Michael Damian gets more than he bargained for in Christine Scott's *Imitation Bride*. Lacey Keegan was only pretending to be his fiancée, but now that wedding plans were snowballing, he began wishing that their make-believe romance was real.

Two more stories with humor and love round out the month in *Second Chance at Marriage* by Pamela Dalton, and *An Improbable Wife* by debut author Sally Carleen.

Happy Reading!

Anne Canadeo

Senior Editor, Silhouette Romance

Please address questions and book requests to:
Silhouette Reader Service
U.S.: 3010 Walden Ave., P.O. Box 1325, Buffalo, NY 14269
Canadian: P.O. Box 609, Fort Erie, Ont. L2A 5X3

COWBOY
FOR HIRE

Dorsey Kelley

Silhouette
R O M A N C E™
Published by Silhouette Books
America's Publisher of Contemporary Romance

I dedicate this novel to the entire ranching Twisselman family of California. On your cattle drives you've helped me, taught me and laughed at me when I wore my spurs backwards—not easy to do! Someday I'll get everything right and show you all. In the meantime...Yeehaw!

  SILHOUETTE BOOKS

ISBN 0-373-19098-0

COWBOY FOR HIRE

Copyright © 1995 by Dorsey Adams

Allen County Public Library
900 Webster Street
PO Box 2270
Fort Wayne, IN 46801-2270

Printed in U.S.A.

Books by Dorsey Kelley

Silhouette Romance

Montana Heat #714
Lone Star Man #863
Texas Maverick #900
Wrangler #938
The Cowboy's Proposal #997
Cowboy for Hire #1098

DORSEY KELLEY

can hardly get off a horse long enough to write books.
She helps ranchers move cattle around in annual drives,
participates in roundups and brandings, and hams it up
in parades. Now, she is learning to team rope because,
she says, "It's so much darn fun!"

When she isn't horsing around, Dorsey plays tennis,
takes her three small daughters to the mall and makes
her husband crazy with planning ever more ranch trips.

Dear Reader,

What could be more thrilling than to be swept into the hard-muscled arms of a compelling man? Especially when said man has honed those muscles in the labor of helping animals grow and making land produce? Who could be sexier than a man who understands the value of hard work and reward—and wants nothing more than to share those rewards with the woman in his life?

Cowboys live this difficult life every day. It may surprise some that this is what I find sexy about cowboys and about the Western life-style. It's not so much the jauntily cocked Stetson, worn jeans and boots, although these, too, when wrapped around a good-looking man, are reason enough for any redblooded woman to get hot and bothered.

For me, it's the tiny wrinkles around his eyes, earned from staring at distant sun-filled horizons. It's his ability to find something positive in even the most devastating calamity, to shrug off adversity and forge ahead in the face of defeat. Even more, it's his wealth of human knowledge, of commitment to the land and to one special woman that you can discern if you bother to search. So, the next time you meet with a cowboy, look deep into his eyes. You'll see what I mean.

Dorsey Kelly

Chapter One

From under the brim of his beat-up cowboy hat, Bent Murray glanced around the overcrowded arena grounds and snorted in disgust. Dust clouds kicked up by city slicker boots, the smell of popcorn and burned hot dogs, shrill crying children, scantily dressed young women posturing behind the chutes hoping to catch a cowboy's eye—it was all too much.

A Los Angeles rodeo.

He hated California smog, traffic, short tempers, conmen. Too many rats in a cage, in his opinion. A man needed space—open country—where he could breathe. As soon as he could, he'd collect Sarah and hit the road for Montana high country. He'd buy a fair-size ranch, run a few hundred Angus, raise lightning-fast quarter horses.

It was a wonderful fantasy, a dream to comfort him when he felt the oppressive atmosphere of fast-paced southern California clamp down.

But for now, there were horses to shoe. With a resigned sigh, he hung the scarred leather apron around his waist, grabbed up hoof nippers and bent to the task.

"Mr. Murray?"

The female voice sounded somewhere above Bent's left ear. He grimaced at the intrusion.

"I need you, Murray," she insisted.

A live one, he thought with weary cynicism. In his younger, rodeo days, when a girl made such a suggestive remark, he would never let her get away. Not until he'd had his fill of her.

The old days were ancient history.

Now, as he stooped over, holding a colt's forefoot between his knees, with a hammer in one hand and a brace of nails clamped between his teeth, he wondered impatiently why people always waited until he was in this awkward position to bother him.

Well, *he* couldn't be bothered looking up. "Yeah?" he said through the nails.

The girl moved closer, and into the line of his lowered vision came a pair of slim legs in scuffed and scarred boots and worn jeans. She held a bay horse on a lead rope. Right away he noticed that the horse had been badly shod. This girl probably wanted him to wave a magic wand and cure her horse's problem, whatever it was. The worst horse owners were teenage girls—they loved their horses like precious pets and figured they knew worlds more than a professional farrier. Such clients often made his life miserable by demanding unreasonable and crazy remedies to their darlings' hoof problems.

"Murray?" she persisted. "Please."

Bent sighed. Slowly he straightened his stiff back, letting the hoof down to examine the girl—who wasn't a girl at all as he'd first supposed, but a small, slender woman. Her anxious expression couldn't hide the prettiness of her bright hazel green eyes or the golden color of her braid beneath her straw cowboy hat. Not late teens, he thought, revising her age. Early twenties?

Nevertheless, a small stab of disappointment arrowed through him. Bent was thirty-eight himself; she was too young for him. He leaned his tough, callused hand against the horse's flank and ignored his aching back. "You need me, huh?"

Her gaze flickered. "My, uh, horse does." She gestured behind her to the brown-coated mare. "I've heard you're the best farrier around. Sierra needs the best if she and I are going to win the World."

Bent raised one skeptical brow. "Gonna win the World, huh? Barrel racing?"

She drew herself up proudly and stroked the nose of her horse. "We want it all."

"Lotta competition."

She shrugged. "Sierra's great."

His gaze skimmed the bay's muscled-up hindquarters, the straight, strong tendons and alert eyes. "Nice looker."

For the first time, the woman smiled. "Thanks."

"What's your name?" Bent's eyes lingered on her mouth, her straight white teeth, shapely lips and the light dusting of freckles sprinkled on her cheeks.

"Kate Monahan." She faced him squarely, without artifice. He liked that. His glance drifted downward, over the hollow of her throat and the rising of her breasts beneath her plain, Western-cut shirt. Her shirt was open at the throat, and at her chest he noticed that one of the pearlized buttons was slipping free of its buttonhole. If the thing came open, would he get a glimpse of cleavage? Was the display deliberate?

He walked to the horse, ran his hands down its legs where the brown coat turned black, and lifted its hooves. Carefully, he inspected each, holding the hard hooves against his leather-aproned knees until he was satisfied. At last he faced the woman. "This mare shouldn't be used, Kate. She's got a quarter crack on her right front and maybe a light case of navicular disease. You race her all year and she's gonna go lame."

"No!" Kate snapped, and stepped forward to grab his forearm. At the touch of her fingers he went tense with awareness and his eyes narrowed in surprise. "Sierra has everything it takes," Kate said urgently. "There isn't a faster horse on the circuit—and she's got heart. She's always done whatever I've asked of her and more. It's just her hooves..." She faltered, licked her lips and started again. "She needs care. *You* can give it to her. You are the best, aren't you?"

Bent looked down into Kate's wide hazel gaze and felt stirring sexual interest. Well, who wouldn't, with her big eyes pleading and her hanging on to his arm like that? He wondered if she had a boyfriend. Not that it mattered.

Next to her he felt old, jaded. Kate had an innocent freshness that made him think of things hopeful, like spring flowers and young love.

He pivoted so that her hand fell away. With his fingers at the mare's soft muzzle, he inserted his thumb into its mouth, gently pried it open and took seconds to inspect the teeth, which revealed age.

"Your mare's getting on, too. What is she? Sixteen? Seventeen?"

"Almost seventeen. But she's in great shape," she said defensively.

"Uh-huh." He watched for a moment as the mare nuzzled the woman's shoulder. "And that heart you say she's got is why. She wants to please you. But you may be working her beyond her ability."

Kate firmed her mouth. "Will you help us or not? I know her feet are going to need a lot of attention. I can pay." She added this last with a note of desperation.

Despite himself, he felt a response to her helplessness and cursed inwardly. It came from something deep inside he couldn't control—a primitive chemical reaction of a male sensing need in a female. A need only he could fulfill.

Something very much like a male answering the cry of his mate.

He'd never been stupid about women. At least not since Alicia. He wouldn't start now.

"Sure, I'll shoe your horse. Why not? None of my business if you run her into the ground."

Without waiting for a reply he brushed by her. He collected his hammer, placed the nails back in his mouth and told her in a muffled voice, "Come back later. Around three o'clock."

Ignoring her, he carefully pounded five nails through the shoe into the hoof wall, then twisted off the sharp points with the claw end of his hammer.

"What's your first name?" Kate asked suddenly, and he squinted up at her from his position.

"Thought you'd left," he said discouragingly.

"Not yet," she retorted, and he had to admire her tenacity. She was peering at him like she was trying to place him. His heart began to sink and he averted his face. She leaned toward him. "So, what's your name?"

"Benton," he growled.

"Benton Murray." She rolled the name around and even without glancing up he knew the exact moment when dawning recognition widened her eyes. "I thought you looked familiar. You—I know who you are—"

"A farrier," he supplied dryly. "You know—a horse-shoer?"

"No, I mean who you *used* to be."

He winced and braced himself.

She was excited now, her words tumbling over themselves. "Benton Murray—All-Around World Champion Cowboy. Bull rider and bareback bronc. Back in . . . was it '81 or '82?"

He caught up another tool and clinched the hooves. "Can't remember."

"I think it was '81. My dad was so excited—we were there at Oklahoma City when you rode that bronc on the last day of the Finals. The scores between you and the other riders were so close, but in the last go-round you were the only one who stuck on for the full time. The crowd went wild—even my dad jumped up yelling for you and spilled my soda."

Bent turned his head sideways to give her a wry glance. "Spilled your soda, huh? Sorry. I'll buy you another sometime."

"Sure." She was looking at him with a mixture of awe and reverence—an expression he hadn't seen cross a woman's face since the height of his rodeo days. Back then, he had considered women's adulation his due and had taken full advantage of it. Now, it just made him uneasy.

"Look, I'm busy," he said a bit more gruffly than he'd intended. "I've got a lot of work. Bring your mare back at three."

"Bent Murray," she repeated, and he wondered if she'd heard him. "I can't believe it. You're a world champion—the real thing. This is an honor. Maybe you could help me, give me pointers."

"Forget it." He shook his head and drew in a deep breath. She was bending toward him, her hands braced on her knees. Suddenly he noticed that the button had worked free and he did indeed see a shadowed valley at the tops of her breasts.

Was she coming on to him? Accordingly, his body reacted. She was young, possibly willing; in his mind she was already beneath him, hips undulating as he pleasured her.

Yeah, sure.

He shrugged off the vivid images and gritted his teeth against his body's tightening. Had he become an aging lecher, lusting after sweet, innocent girls? Why would a pretty thing like her look at him? He was just a lowly horseshoer now. A nobody. Nothing.

Some might say he was wasting his life, his talents, doing this menial work and nothing more. But he'd made his peace with himself long ago, hadn't he?

"Forget it," he repeated harshly.

She made no move to leave and suddenly he lost patience. He stood up so fast the horse spooked and threw up its head. Automatically, he put out a soothing hand and rubbed its withers.

With an effort he controlled his voice, but still the words sounded short, bitten off. "Look, I *was* a world champion a long time ago. Fourteen years ago. Now I make my living beneath the tail of a horse. Got it? I can't help you, I can't help anybody."

He disliked seeing her thrilled smile fade, but he forced himself to go on. "I've got no more time for you right now, Katie girl, so git."

She did not. But he noticed her flush heightened and she appeared to dig her heels into the hard-packed earth. "I remember you used to offer rodeo schools—that you even helped a few barrel racers win titles. What about Maria Vendala? You coached her, didn't you? Turned her from a good barrel racer into the greatest champion rodeo's ever seen." She licked her lips. "I need a trainer, Murray. You come to a lot of rodeos, anyway, tending horses, don't you?"

"No," he said.

"You'd be perfect for the job," she went on. "You could train me."

He stared at her in disbelief. "You've got to be kidding."

"I'll make it worth your while. You'll get a percentage of my purses. I know most barrel racers don't have formal trainers. But think about it. You need money, don't you?"

He felt his face darken. How did she know? "What do you mean?" he asked grimly.

"Well, everybody needs money."

"You're crazy, you know that? And if you don't leave me alone, I won't be able to take you at three, either."

"All right," she said so obediently he sent her a sharp glance, sharp enough to see the flash of rebellion in her eyes. She turned to go. "I'll be back at three. By the end of this year Sierra and I will have enough winnings to qualify for Nationals. We'll win the World, Murray."

The note of conviction in her words gave him pause. He didn't think she could win—not without experience. And not with that aging horse who was ready to come up lame. He hadn't seen Kate perform, but her youthful bravado was good. It might take her pretty far; champions needed a touch of arrogance to succeed. They needed to believe they were better than others; they needed hunger to drive them on through rodeo's many adversities—slow, losing score times, horse trouble, injuries and financial woes.

The woman had spunk, he'd admit that. And it was the kind of open-faced, eager honesty that drew men. Being new on the circuit and easy on the eyes, she'd field plenty of offers.

Rodeo cowboys weren't as shy as people believed. The young waddies he knew would descend on this one like a pack of starving coyotes.

Bent watched her walk away, heading toward a beat-up one-horse trailer and rusted pickup truck. She was slender, but her hips and thighs were rounded and feminine. Her breasts, though not large, were high and youthful.

Young.

Too young for him.

Bent forced himself to resume his task. He'd tend her horse and those of his other clients and continue stashing away the money—as he had been doing for years—until he had enough to buy that spread in Montana. Then he could finally be a real daddy to Sarah. God knew his mom was getting too old to raise an active twelve-year-old.

As if thinking of his daughter could conjure her up, she appeared before him, sipping cola from a straw. As always when he saw Sarah, he felt his tension easing. She was the single bright light in his life, his only source of joy.

"How're you doin', Sport?" he asked.

She smiled, showing orthodontic braces he'd worked overtime to afford. "Good, Daddy. I watched the barrel racing this morning. It was so exciting—"

"Don't get any ideas," he warned.

"Dad." She drew out the word. "I wouldn't get hurt. I just want to try—"

"No. We're not a rodeoing family, so forget it. But..." he relented, "I'm shoeing one of the barrel racer's horses later. You can come talk to her."

Sarah's brown eyes shone. With an impatient movement, she swept back her ill-cut hair, which hung unevenly about her shoulders. "Thanks, Dad. I'll come back."

She raced off to watch the bull riding and he smiled. She had such pretty eyes. He wished she'd get rid of her baggy jeans, wear something more girlish. He'd buy her something if he knew where to go or what to get.

Shrugging, Bent put the notion from his mind. Sarah had no mother and he wasn't cut out for the role. Even his mother, with whom Sarah lived most of the time, didn't fuss over the girl's appearance.

He thought about Kate Monahan and her neat braid and well-fitting denims. She had a dream of winning the World? Well, he'd already done that—much good it had done him. Now he was just a has-been, a solitary horseshoer picking up a hundred bucks here, two hundred there, and saving his money. Always saving. For Sarah. For a home.

Bent straightened to get a bar shoe with low calks and hesitated a moment while the pain in his lower back predictably bore down, then receded. From the corner of his eye he saw Kate Monahan toss her hat aside, then stake her horse under a live oak so it could graze on a bit of grass after the morning's perform- ance. Sunlight dappled through the tree branches and fell on Kate's blond hair, burnishing it to spun gold. She stroked her horse's sleek neck and suddenly looked over her shoulder directly at him.

Their eyes met across the forty-some yards and Bent felt the impact of feminine yearning she directed at him like an anvil blow to his gut. This was no little girl pin- ing for a boyfriend, he realized. Kate Monahan was a fully mature woman—younger than him, yes, but a woman nonetheless, who wanted a man. Him. She wanted him.

He stared, unable to break the band of awareness that strung between them.

Again he heard a cry. Somewhere in his conscious- ness, in a shadowy place deep in his psyche, emotions roused. From a powerful well of loneliness he rarely acknowledged, a wail of need and desire echoed, shiv- ering up his spine to rest heavily in his chest.

He shuddered, fighting . . . fighting down the im- pulses that urged him to pursue this woman, to ride her down and take her so that the restlessness deep in his soul would be silenced, at least for a time.

He knew that, at best, it would be for only a short while, because the separation, the aloneness, always returned to haunt him.

Deliberately he turned his back on her, shutting her out and hoping she would get it. He was not avail- able—either as a horse trainer or as a man.

Any part of him once available had died long ago. Back in the time when he'd failed to defend his title and failed to hold Alicia's love. It was the year after he'd won National Finals. The hated memory burned in his gut. He'd never been the same.

He certainly had nothing to offer a rodeo-obsessed female with hopeful eyes and sweet curves, and whose years numbered little more than half his own. Nothing. He had a solid goal for which he'd been working years. He'd get that ranch, by damn. And he wouldn't miss any more of the milestones in Sarah's life. No starry-eyed *girl* like Kate with a heart full of naive dreams would be allowed to distract him.

Kate Monahan carefully ran her hands down Sierra's black-hued legs, feeling for "stocked up" hocks that would indicate swelling or soreness, and was relieved when she noticed none.

Sierra was getting older, as Benton Murray had pointed out. Benton Murray. Kate threw another glance at where he was working on a sorrel quarter horse. For a quiet man, there were needs in him simmering just beneath the surface. She could sense them.

Just at that moment he looked at her again and she experienced the same shock of fascination she'd felt while speaking to him. Perhaps it was the unusual amber shade of his eyes that intrigued her. Once or twice before she'd seen the same color, but always on people with freckled or very fair skin.

Murray's skin was tanned dark and the hair that showed under the edges of his silver-belly gray hat was a thick, untrimmed brown. His shoulders were wide, strong, capable. His legs were long and athletic, hardened with muscle. He would be a magnificent lover.

Kate gasped at her thoughts. How would she know what kind of lover he'd make? Her, a woman of practically no experience with men. Anyway, she would never get the opportunity to find out. She was not in the market for a bedmate.

Maybe it was his quiet assurance that attracted her. No—*attracted* was the wrong word. Interested, maybe, but not in a relationship sort of way. He was a former world champion rodeo rider and, as such, of course she was interested in him. She might have had a crush on him as a teenager, but that had been a childish infatuation. She was drawn to all rodeo champions, past and present, because they could help her, impart their knowledge, teach her what she was so desperate to learn.

How to win.

A sixth sense she'd always had and always trusted whispered insistently that Bent Murray was the answer to her prayers. He was *right* for her. He had the experience, the knowledge, the ability to make her what she had to be. A winner.

Only by winning could she earn the income necessary to keep Mimi in comfort during her later years.

Bent could help her earn what she so craved: a financially worry-free future. Mimi's money would last only this one year, and Kate would rather roll up into a saddle blanket and die than let Mimi down.

"Kate!" an eager masculine voice called, and she recognized Flash Johnson, her neighbor in Riverside and, like her, a young rookie on the circuit.

"Flash," she greeted him warmly. "I wondered if I'd see you. Mimi said your mama told her down at Grandon's Grocery you might enter. I'm glad you're here—now I'll know somebody at least."

"Sure." Boyishly, he ducked his hat and thrust his hands into his jeans' front pockets. "I get to all the rodeos I can now, you know." He patted Sierra's neck. "Good luck tomorrow chasing them cans."

She scowled without heat. "It's not chasing cans, Flash, it's barrel racing."

He shrugged, grinning. "Roping's where the real skill is, Kate."

She laid her hand on her chest and batted her eyes. "Goodness, calf roping is ever so much more glamorous than barrel racing. Why, if you tried it, you might scar up your pretty knees on those barrels."

"That's right. But if I mess up my knees it's sure not gonna be from some oil drum. Someday, I'm gonna win the World."

Kate dropped her teasing and leaned toward him. "Do you know that's Benton Murray over there—All-Around Champion of '81?"

Uneasily, the youth glanced at the farrier. "Yeah, I know."

"So, why don't you go talk to him? Get some pointers?"

Flash gave an awkward shrug. "He doesn't really like talking to rookies like me."

She thought about how Murray had warned her off and she pursed her lips. Well, she'd never been one to take no easily. The man must be a mine of information—why wouldn't he share it with hopefuls like her and Flash?

Besides, he could make money off them. Dozens, maybe hundreds of rodeo-crazy kids would pay well to take a clinic from him. It was the way of former champions to offer frequent week-long schools and share the knowledge they could no longer apply themselves. She, herself, planned to happily spend her retirement doing so. Once she had become a champion.

Then she could eventually graduate to former champion and capitalize on her titles.

But first she had to win them.

Just then the sound of crashing hooves on metal pipe railings startled her, and both she and Flash whirled to see a huge Brahman bull kick out a loose pen railing and go thundering out. The red-coated animal was horned, with a dirty white ring around one eye. It headed away from the rodeo grounds and directly down the dirt road, just like a truck driving on the right side of the street.

Kate might have laughed if she hadn't known the danger. Hopefully none of the rodeo crowd were walking that way! Unsure of what they could do, she and Flash raced after the maddened animal, when in the corner of her eye she saw a rider leap onto a saddled buckskin horse, catch up the reins and give chase.

Bent Murray.

He kicked the buckskin into a headlong gallop and Kate watched, amazed, as he jerked down the coiled lariat that hung from the saddle. Swiftly building a loop, he whirled it overhead. In seconds he overtook the Brahma, snagged the animal by the horns and dallied the home end onto the saddle horn. His horse rocked back on its heels and skidded on the hard earth.

The bull twisted around, bucking. It bellowed, enraged. Bent's horse held fast and billowing dust rose to partially obscure other riders coming up to throw additional ropes on the fighting animal until it was subdued.

Kate let out a relieved breath and slumped onto a low split-rail fence. Flash stood, awed, beside her as the men pulled the beast past and put it into a sturdy pen.

"Did you see that, Kate?" Flash asked eagerly. "Did you?"

"Of course I saw, you idiot. I was standing right beside you." She punched his arm.

"Did you see Murray rope that gnarly bull?" In his excitement he recounted the entire event just as if she hadn't been there at all.

Kate listened patiently, amused. But slowly she began to understand.

"Murray's really good—fantastic with a rope. I'd heard he was, but, you know in his heyday he was always a rider. I wonder why he doesn't compete. Man, the way he pulled down that bull was pure poetry."

Kate considered that, and when a few of the other men drifted past, complimenting Murray on his skill, she began to wonder anew about him. If he was so all-fired good at roping, why didn't he participate in the timed events?

She resolved to ask.

At last it was three o'clock and she led Sierra over to the man. He was just finishing up with a big black gelding owned by one of the cowboys. "I've added the support of trailers," Bent said, pointing to extensions sticking out to the side of the hind shoes, "and this'll help his cow-hocked stance."

"That's fine, Bent," the owner said, looking pleased as he began to lead the horse away. "I'll cut you a check straightaway."

Bent turned to face Kate. Behind him, sitting on his truck's open tailgate, was a young girl of about twelve. She wore old, loose jeans and a too-big flannel top. Her hair was a glossy brown but was in no particular style and in fact appeared to have been trimmed with a pair of Bent's wire cutters.

Despite the girl's lack of style, Kate could see her resemblance to Bent. Vaguely she recalled something about his wife's death years back. An accident that had left him with an infant.

Kate glanced at her curiously and the girl dropped her eyes shyly.

Without comment Bent took the lead rope from Kate and put the horse in a set of cross-ties. She watched as he inspected Sierra's hoof angle by kneeling down while looking at the lower front legs from the side. He checked the lateral balance and then straightened to collect tools to trim and shape the hooves.

Working over Sierra, he never once met Kate's gaze but asked several questions about how much the horse was used and under what circumstances. Finally he fell silent, working efficiently. Kate studied him, noted his economy of movement and skill in handling the horse. She made no move to leave.

"You gonna watch?" he asked her suddenly.

"Well . . . yeah. . . . Is it all right?"

He grunted noncommittally then gestured at the girl. "My daughter, Sarah. She wants to meet a real barrel racer."

"Hi, Sarah," Kate said brightly.

"Hi." The girl blushed and Kate smiled to put her at ease. All too well she remembered her preadolescent awkwardness. She turned back to Bent. "I saw you rope that bull," she ventured. "You were great."

Another grunt.

"He really could have hurt somebody—mowed down some little kids, maybe. But you just jumped onto that horse and lit out. Whose horse was that, anyway?''

"Friend of mine's. Ty Banning.''

"Oh." She knew Ty was a top roper on the circuit. "Anyway, Flash Johnson—he's a new kid—is a terrific roper and he was impressed with you.''

Bent turned his head sideways and for the first time looked at her. She noticed his mouth was firmed up tight, like it would be if he were holding nails, but he wasn't now. His face looked hard, forbidding. "I'm gonna trim back the heel side of this quarter crack so it bears no weight, then apply a pad and a bar shoe. That should help distribute your mare's weight evenly around the rest of the hoof.''

"Okay," Kate said. "About the roping. Flash and I were wondering... That is, well, I know you're too old to ride the roughstock." She noticed his scowl and hurried on. "But a question comes to mind." She waited and when he didn't respond, she pressed ahead. "Why, if you're such a good roper, don't you compete?''

He made a movement with his shoulder that she supposed was a shrug. "Don't want to.''

"Why?''

Bent shook his head and threw aside a hoof rasp. Slowly he stood up, putting a hand to his lower back for a moment. "You're a pushy little thing, aren't you?''

She drew a breath. "My grandma always told me persistence pays off.''

"You sure she didn't say it 'ticks people off'?''

"Don't tell me if you don't want to. I was just curious." She hunched a shoulder away.

"I've got a feeling you won't quit until I give you something to chew on." He captured her gaze and held it, and she could see dim fires of anger starting to burn in the amber depths of his eyes. "I don't want to rodeo. Not riding, not roping, not steer wrestling. I'm just here to work—to make money and go home."

"You could make money training me."

He let out a mirthless laugh. "We're back to that, huh?"

"I'm good, Bent," she told him softly. "And I'm trainable. I can take instruction—I'm learning all the time. But I need a top-notch trainer. You. I need you."

Though Kate knew her comments might be construed as innuendo, she wasn't prepared for the flare of sexuality that came to life in Bent's eyes. She took an unconscious step back and sucked in a breath. An unwilling thrill of awareness shot from her toes to her nape. "I—I didn't mean—"

"Didn't mean what?" Suddenly he twisted to face Sarah, who was avidly observing them. Digging into his jeans' pocket, he said, "Sarah, honey, go get me a soda, huh?"

She got up. "Sure." And taking the money, she walked toward the concession stand.

When she was yards away, Bent advanced on Kate, capturing her gaze with an intensity she found mesmerizing and frightening. He was taller than she'd thought, and a bit of curling chest hair escaped at the throat of his Western shirt. Would it be crisp to her fingers? Or soft?

A low thundering started in her pulse, raced through her limbs and made her breath short. He came closer, so close she could smell his odors of horse and leather and a scent uniquely masculine, uniquely his. Like pine trees at high mountain altitudes.

Without warning he reached out a callused hand and cupped her chin. Looking down into her eyes, he lowered his voice. "Maybe you're too young to know how to handle men. Here's a tip for you—don't come on so strong. Some will run off, be intimidated by a woman like you. But others—real men—will be challenged."

She swallowed and knew he felt the movement of her throat. Her heart seemed to have stopped beating.

"They'll chase till they catch you," he finished. "You'll be like a henhouse chick caught by a hungry wolf."

"I can take care of myself."

He looked skeptical.

She jerked her chin away and glared at him. Suddenly she was angry, too. "All your talk of challenges—why don't you have any? You have at least two valuable skills you don't even use. You're one of the best ropers I've ever seen, but you don't want that. You could be a great trainer, but you say no. Why don't you rise to at least one of the challenges, Bent?" She rushed on, blurting out whatever came to mind without thinking. "Make it be me—and Sierra. Stay overnight and watch me ride tomorrow. Draw your own conclusions. If we don't have the talent, then go."

He pivoted away, back to the horse. "No."

She stared at his profile, frustrated. He was so bullheaded and blind!

Then a thought began forming. As she looked at him, observed his closed expression and taut jawline, she wondered if her hunch could be correct.

"You're scared, aren't you?" she whispered.

He whirled. "What?"

"Something...something here. At the rodeo. Is it the bulls? The bucking horses?"

He guffawed. "*Old* as I am," he said sarcastically, "I can still ride any bull or horse."

"Then, what? Are you afraid of failure? I remember the year after you won the championship, you didn't cut it the next. Then you quit."

"So? Lotta guys quit after a while." His expression went carefully blank and sent off warning bells in Kate's mind. He was lying. Why she was so attuned to this particular man, she didn't know, but she could feel his tension. His unrest.

"Watch me," she dared him quietly. "Stay overnight. I'll bet Sarah would like to," she added slyly— and felt a small triumph when she saw him hesitate. "Watch me ride tomorrow." Coming up, she touched his shoulder and felt him go still. He was warm beneath his shirt. Warm and alive. Muscular.

In that moment something changed. Later, Kate tried to interpret the difference in him, to understand it. But she couldn't.

Slowly he turned and gave her a hard-eyed stare that held her captive. With excruciating care he raked her body with his eyes. It took all her willpower to remain still beneath the onslaught, but she felt the amber heat of his gaze sear her thighs and breasts. Lordy, did she feel it.

"What would you pay?" he wondered idly, his gruff voice ruffling her nerve endings. "If I watch you, think you have the stuff, and agree to train you, what would you be willing to sacrifice?"

She paled, but didn't pretend to misunderstand him. "Money, of course. Not that much, but it should be enough."

He was shaking his head before she finished. "Maybe I want something else. Maybe it's your youth. Your enthusiasm. Something I've lost."

She swallowed heavily and searched for a way out even while knowing there would be none. She was frightened and intrigued all at once, as if she were teetering on the edge of a towering cliff. On one side was safety and solid ground, on the other, a terrifying fall into darkness. "H-how would a person give those things to another? How could I transfer that to you?"

"You want a trainer—go hire one. You want a championship—enter the event and do your best. I can't guarantee success. I can't guarantee anything."

Her voice was faint, breathy. "I know."

"I'll stay over the night, Kate. I'll watch you tomorrow. If you're good enough, maybe I'll take you on, teach you. But my price is high. Probably too high."

Kate closed her eyes and felt dizzy. Her throat was dry as dust and she swallowed again, this time convulsively. She thought of all she could gain. Then of all she must give up.

She thought of her entire future, Mimi's well-being, her plans for their life. Slowly she opened her eyes and gripped the chain of the cross-ties between white-knuckled fingers.

His expression was fierce, intense. Yet there was something deep in his eyes that she couldn't place...a waiting...a yearning...a bleakness inside him like a frozen winter. Could this man ever be reached? Could a mere woman ever touch his heart?

"You know what my price is, don't you, Kate?" he
asked.
   She couldn't blink, couldn't speak, couldn't breathe.
"A night with me. All night."

"You know I'll buy you a drink," said Kate.

and
so seemed tough, scaring a grizzle of [...]
"A deal is one of all."

Chapter Two

Kate Monahan was good. *Damn* good. Bent thumbed his hat onto the back of his head and drew a deep, long breath, belatedly realizing his mistake as he watched her round the barrels on her brown lightning bolt of a horse. He still couldn't quite believe she'd turned the tables on his outrageous dare. He'd thrown out that challenge about sleeping with him, never dreaming she'd go for it. And she hadn't.

In fact, when she could get her breath, she'd flown into an outraged fury. But she hadn't walked away. Quickly, she'd come up with an alternative. "In exchange for training me part-time, I'll give you a percentage of my winnings *and* help with Sarah."

He remembered frowning, confused. "I don't need any help with Sarah."

"Don't you?" she'd asked with an inscrutably feminine expression. "She needs a woman's influence—maybe somebody closer to her age than her grandma.

She's in puberty, in case it's escaped your notice. Are you prepared to answer the difficult questions?''

Kate had hit a nerve, and she'd known it instantly. He *had* been at a loss with his growing daughter. Before he could reply, she'd pressed her advantage. She'd gone on to explain how she knew what it was like growing up without a mother, how she would have appreciated having someone young, but not judgmental, to help during the awkward years.

Bent rubbed his jaw. Well, his original deal would never have seen fruition anyway, he decided. Kate would probably quit before the year was out. Or her horse would break down.

But, *damn*, in the rodeo arena she was good. He squinted through the sunlight. At his side, Sarah watched with breathless wonder and admiration as Kate passed the electronic timer and finished in excellent time.

When they'd first spoken yesterday, he'd imagined Kate was a competent rider with a so-so horse. Yet now in the afternoon sunlight glinting over the arena, he was being shown—in hoof-thundering, dust-billowing detail—the error of his ways. Who would figure that the sweet, too-young-looking girl could ride like her hair was on fire? Who would guess that the unprepossessing bay mare could run like she'd been shot out of a cannon—a very large, very powerful cannon?

An unwilling chuckle escaped Bent as he mentally kicked himself. Kate and her horse had loads of talent. Yet it was raw talent; she did need help to continue progressing, she was right about that. What got him was that the teacher in him responded to that talent. He could see that woman and horse were a trainer's dream. And he knew without doubt that he *could* help her—make her better, maybe the best there ever was. But should he?

Bent draped his arms over the second arena rail, squinting through rising dust and glare to watch as Kate took her triumphant, winning ride around the arena while the spectators cheered her victory. Beside him, Sarah whooped and waved. He breathed in and sharp, familiar odors from the bull pen mingled with cigarette smoke and sweating horses, hot dogs and nachos with cheese—all scents of a rodeo going full blast. How well Bent remembered, even though he'd long made it a policy to stay away.

Visions of crazy broncs he'd ridden to a standstill, of bulls snorting fire down his neck and of injuries he'd suffered, of parties that lasted well into the night—it all flooded back. *Rodeo*. Was he going to let Kate drag him back into this world?

As Kate cantered by where he waited at the chutes— a streak of purple and turquoise-yoked shirt and tight jeans—she took off her hat and waved to the crowd. Her gaze caught his and her eyes flashed, her triumphant grin telling him more clearly than any words, "See, cowboy? I *told* you I was good."

Bent watched her closely. Her shirt flattened on her chest, outlining her high breasts. She was breathless and glowing with feminine vitality, and he stared, unable to look away. His body helplessly reacted. He wanted this female, and he wanted her *bad*.

For no reason at all Bent felt his throat tightening, felt the irritating prod of guilt. Kate Monahan was young, on her way to a wide-open future in barrel racing—maybe even fame. Perhaps it wasn't right, what he wanted.

Guilt settled in his gut like a stack of horseshoes, and he tried to shake it off. But it wouldn't shake. Instead, it made him angry. Kate Monahan really wasn't a girl, he reminded himself. Despite her freckles and slight frame, she was a woman grown, fully cognizant of what she was getting into. He'd be a fool not to take advantage of such a deal. She'd turned his indecent proposal down flat, but Bent had lived too many years not to know that the simmering, volatile sexual energy that hummed between them would not go unconsummated. Sooner or later, they'd enjoy a hell of a romp in bed.

He sought her out, finding her where she'd ridden behind the chutes and was receiving accolades from others. Her brilliantly colored outfit made her easy to spot. When she spied him, her smile widened and his breath caught. She raced to him, put a hand on his chest, and his breath caught again.

"So? What do you think?" she asked eagerly.

Unable to help himself, he reached out, his hand going low on her back, almost touching her derriere, and pulled her flush against his side so that her breasts flattened on the hard plane of his rib cage. He grinned wolfishly. Maybe things would work out to his liking. Yes, indeed, maybe they would. "Lady," he drawled, staring down into her wide eyes, "you've got yourself a trainer."

"Come on, Sierra," Kate shouted into the rushing wind, hoping her racing mare could hear her. They rounded the first two barrels in a cloverleaf pattern and bolted for the third. Kate encouraged the horse, knees clamped tight, voice whispering now, hugging low to heaving withers. "Come *on.*"

It might be a weed-sprinkled field next to Mimi's house. The oil drums she'd placed at precise intervals might be battered and feature peeling paint logos from long defunct petroleum companies, but in Kate's mind she was in a formal rodeo arena, the announcer blaring her name over the loudspeaker. The barrels were slick and painted instead of old, the ground soft dirt instead of weeds. Crowds watched eagerly, urged her on, urged her horse to tuck tighter around the corners. Kate leaned lower still and felt her hat whip off in the wind created by their headlong rush.

Blowing air forced tears to Kate's eyes but there was no time to wipe them away—no time for anything save exhorting Sierra to turn sharper, stretch her long legs that extra inch, an inch to buy them a tenth of a second, all the difference in the world.

Rodeo was a fever in her blood. Kate loved the color, the excitement, the bonding of human and beast working together in competition. Beneath her, Sierra ran dead hard, her hooves churning out dirt clods, crushing dandelions. The mare put her heart and soul into running, for the pure joy of the sport, and much of that joy communicated to Kate. Man, she thought, they were flying.

They rounded the last barrel and Kate's knee glanced off the hard metal side. The barrel teetered, then fell over. Ignoring the pain, Kate reined Sierra into the final stretch and they shot past the faded old cone placed on the ground.

Mimi punched the large stopwatch with her thumb and squinted at the dial. "That's better," she said. "Much better."

Pulling Sierra to a sliding stop, Kate trotted her back to where her grandmother waited by the cone. Mimi wore loose, faded jeans and soft boots. Like Kate, she was small, her eyes the same lively hazel.

"It's better," Kate allowed. "But not good enough. I'm having trouble with Sierra cutting too close on the last barrel. We knocked it clean down—that would cost a five-second penalty I can't afford. Am I leaning over and don't know it?"

Mimi lifted one thin shoulder. "I didn't see you lean. But then, my eyes aren't what they used to be. Maybe your new trainer can help."

Slowly, Kate nodded. She hoped Bent would be worth the cost she was paying—in money as well as in other ways. Kate frowned, a tiny shiver running through her as she wondered for the hundredth time if she'd done the right thing. Sarah she already liked. But had Bent fully accepted that she would *not* sleep with him as part of their deal?

Mimi peered at the stopwatch again. "In my day, this would have won any class." She shook her graying curls and sighed. "It really isn't enough for today's competition. Do you think your trainer can lower your time?"

"He'd better, for what he's getting," Kate muttered, rubbing her sore knee.

"Oh, dear." Mimi's eyes clouded. "Is he so expensive?"

"Don't worry," Kate hurried on, guessing her grandmother's financial concerns. "I've cut a deal with him. He's taking only ten percent of my purses, which means he has even more incentive to help me win. Ten percent of nothing is nothing." She shrugged.

"But how is it you managed to talk a professional trainer into such a low amount? And ... you say it's a man?"

Kate bit her lip and busied herself with patting Sierra's gleaming neck. "Actually, his name's Benton Murray, a former All-Around Champion from years back. And...he hasn't trained anyone in a long time—he's a farrier now. Also, he won't travel with me, but will meet me every few weeks."

"Still," Mimi said slowly, her perceptive ears hearing more than Kate was comfortable with, "ten percent seems awfully low to train someone."

"Don't worry about it," Kate said quickly, wanting to get off the subject. "The details are all worked out. Time me again, won't you?"

"Flash's here," Mimi said. "He can do it while I check the coffee cake." She held the stopwatch out to the approaching red-haired youth.

"Hi, Flash," Kate called out, smiling. She'd always liked the young man who lived down the street. He had little home life and Mimi had practically raised him—seeing that he had a good lunch for school each day, giving him chores to perform for pocket money. "Right that barrel, please? And watch me this run to see if I'm leaning in on the last one, okay?"

Flash grinned and ran over to right the battered drum.

While she waited, her mind turned to Bent Murray. They'd made arrangements for Bent to meet her at three-week intervals as she traveled the circuit. That way, he'd be able to care for Sierra's hooves as well as train Kate.

With a few days free, Kate had loaded her mare into the trailer and driven back to Riverside, to the small clapboard house she shared with Mimi.

Flash ran up to hand Kate her hat. "When'd you get back, Kate?" he asked, blue eyes sparkling and welcoming. "I stopped by yesterday but Mimi said you were getting in late."

Kate sighed and swung down. "Midnight," she said when she was on the ground. "I'm a little tired." Facing Flash, she touched his arm. "How's your mom?"

The brief hesitation told the story. She didn't need the small hints of his tightening jaw, the echo of anguish in his light eyes. "Still drinking?" she asked softly.

He dropped his head to his chest and stirred the dirt with the toe of his worn boot. "I've been wondering, Kate. Maybe you could help me sort something out?" Normally Flash was outgoing, upbeat, but now he appeared unnaturally serious.

"Sure." She wiped at Sierra's sweaty flank and remembered Bent's admonition not to overwork the horse. Her own faded plaid shirt was damp with perspiration. "I guess Sierra's had enough anyway. Help me put her up?"

They walked together to cool the horse, then went on to the dilapidated barn, unsaddled Sierra and washed her down. Kate said nothing, allowing the boy time to marshal his thoughts. Finally he said, "I've been thinking about, uh, the future."

From beneath Sierra's neck, Kate craned a look at him. "The future?"

"Yeah." He shifted his weight from foot to foot. "I mean, like . . . a real job. You know—like a career?"

"But you're roping, aren't you?" As soon as she said the words, she knew the problem.

"Uh, it doesn't exactly pay the bills unless you win." He frowned and she knew he seldom won. Suddenly he looked the slightest bit desperate. "Kate, I've got a small savings I'm using this season to rodeo. But I really need something steady I can count on to make a living—for Ma and me."

At mention of his mother, all fell into place. "I see," Kate replied slowly. Flash's father had passed away years before and his mother's slow slide into alcohol dependency was sad. She wouldn't stop drinking, wouldn't see what her addiction was doing to her only son.

Now, Flash's maturity for so young a man touched Kate. He was barely eighteen, yet she saw immediately that he was right to worry.

"What will I do, Kate?" He looked at his hands as if he might find the answer written across his palms. Kate's heart sank. She didn't see how she could help him—she was giving everything she had to try to cement the future for her own small family of Mimi and herself.

Troubled, she forced herself to smile at him confidently. "I'm not sure yet. But I'll think on it, okay?"

He nodded. "Thanks."

Maybe when she was rich and famous she could hire him to work on her ranch. The one she'd buy with all her money.

Kate ducked her head. Right now she *had* no money. Or at least only enough to subsidize this one year on the circuit. With a good portion of Mimi's capital, she'd put a hefty down payment on an almost-new pickup truck and good hauling trailer for her horse. It was not a cheap investment, but necessary to carry her all over the western United States for the next year.

Biting her lip, she felt doubts assail her. What if she failed? What if she didn't win enough, didn't qualify for Finals? What if Sierra became injured—what if *she* did? All Mimi's small nest egg would be gone; then she'd be in the same position as Flash.

Her own mother had died when she was small, and her father when she was fourteen. Mimi had raised her, nurtured her, much as she was doing for Flash. But at seventeen Kate hadn't the money for college, either. She had her high school diploma, and she could type. If she failed now, she'd have to go back to her low-paying receptionist job.

Kate stared at the bridle in her hands and knew the chill brushing the back of her neck had nothing to do with the cool breeze wafting through the pasture.

"Kate?" Flash inquired.

"What? Oh, I was just woolgathering, thinking about...barrel racing." She threw her free arm around his shoulders and had to go onto her toes because he'd grown a good several inches taller than she was. "Say, could you get off that box so I can give you a real hug?" she teased.

"Okay." He bent his knees and gave her a quick hug. Flash was different from others his age. He wasn't embarrassed to show affection. He was looking past her. "Who's that?"

Twisting to glance over her shoulder, Kate felt a leap in her pulse as she recognized the tall man striding through the field toward her. Bent Murray.

Sunlight framed him from behind, making a silhouette of broad shoulders, slim hips and long, loose-limbed legs. His hat was the same battered silver-belly colored one he'd worn before, and he'd pulled the brim low against the sun's glare. He wore a tan-yoked shirt, jeans with no belt, and scuffed boots. When he reached them, he touched his hat with a thumb and two fingers. His gaze was direct, hard-edged, and missed nothing. "Mornin'."

Kate's throat went dry.

"Hi," Flash said.

"Son." Bent nodded to Flash and turned to inspect the barn. "Nice place, Kate. Lived here all your life?"

"Uh, yes. With my grandmother. She's in the house baking coffee cake." Kate blinked, wondering why she'd added that last bit. It was as if someone else was speaking. Why had he come?

Bent grinned suddenly, his smile very white. "I'm crazy about coffee cake. Think she's got any to spare?"

"Mimi always makes too much," Flash piped up, drawing a frown from Kate. She wasn't sure she wanted the disturbing cowboy hanging around. Making introductions between the two, she smiled ruefully as Flash became predictably impressed. Flash had often listened to her stories of growing up watching rodeo greats—and he knew the tale of when Kate was twelve and watched Bent win the title.

"All-Around Champion," Flash breathed, staring at Bent. His gaze dipped to Bent's midsection. "Why don't you wear your trophy buckle?"

The very fact that the man's face remained expressionless alerted Kate. He'd told her originally he wanted no part of rodeo. Again she wondered why.

Going to the horse still standing in the cross-ties, he lifted Sierra's front hoof and ran his fingers over the small crack. "That buckle's old," he replied. "Gets in the way."

Flash's puzzled glance sought hers, and Kate gave a slight shake of her head. She'd get to the bottom of the mystery, but now wasn't the time. Perhaps she ought to solve the smaller enigma first.

"So, Bent," she began determinedly, "were you in the neighborhood?"

He turned his head and one corner of his mouth lifted. "Yeah. Just driving by."

"Uh-huh." She moved closer to where he was still examining Sierra's hoof. "You hail from Bakersfield, don't you? About, oh, I'd say a three-hour drive away?"

"Three hours?" He pretended to ruminate. "Sounds fair."

"And you were just . . . driving by?"

"Yep." He turned his grin on Flash, who smiled back.

"Bent!" she exclaimed in exasperation. "What are you doing here? I thought we'd agreed to meet in three weeks."

"Oh, that." He straightened, letting Sierra's hoof down. "Didn't I mention that I wanted to inspect your barn—the living conditions for your mare? That has a lot to do with how sound a horse stays, you know. And since Sierra's soundness is mostly my responsibility now, I thought a visit was in order."

"I see." Something in his tone didn't quite ring true. But for the moment she'd play along. "As you can see, my barn's not the best on the market—"

"Might even call it rundown," he noted.

"But it's clean," she said hurriedly. "And well ventilated. When I'm not here, Flash cleans the stall every day and lays fresh shavings. Sierra gets good water and we grain her like the vet told us to."

Bent nodded. "And do you blanket her at night when it's cold?"

"Of course." She blinked. "You see that she's healthy."

"Yeah? Then what's this?" He picked at something high on the horse's dark brown withers and Kate flew to his side.

"What is it?" she cried. "What's wrong?" Up on her toes, she searched the spot but could find nothing amiss. "There's nothing there."

He looked down at her from his superior height and she caught the mischief in his eyes. "Gotcha."

Slowly she relaxed and marveled at this new side to the laconic man. "I didn't know you were the teasing sort," she noted. "I wouldn't ever have guessed it. You've actually got a sense of humor!"

He had the grace to look chagrined. "Guess you haven't been thinking too highly of me."

"It's not that." She shook her head in wonder and moved away. Maybe working with Bent wouldn't be as stressful as she'd imagined. If he could laugh once in a while, she was sure the road would be smoother. To herself, she smiled, secretly delighted. She darted a glance at him and found him watching her with interest. It wouldn't do to let *him* know she was pleased.

It took no effort at all to put a bit of disdain into her voice. "Actually, it shouldn't matter. Just as long as you help me win on Sierra, that's all I care about."

"You will win, Kate." The faith and confidence underlying his tone surprised her and made her small stab at him seem petty. "You've got the right stuff."

"That *stuff* just needs refinement, huh?" She arched a brow at him, feeling easier in his presence than she had before.

"Something like that." He glanced at Flash. "Do you want to check on that coffee cake, son? I like it straight from the oven."

"Me, too!" Flash turned smartly, jogging toward the house.

While Kate watched, Bent ran his hands down each of Sierra's legs, feeling for imperfections or swellings. He said nothing.

After a minute, Kate lost patience. "I thought you'd come to inspect the barn."

"I'm gettin' to it," he said. Slowly he straightened and went into Sierra's stall. He checked the automatic waterer, scuffed his boot through the shavings and down to the stall mat and went over to check the grain bin. "Everything looks good," he finally pronounced.

Kate put one hand on her hip. "That's a relief."

"How'd she run today?" He indicated Sierra.

"Like lightning. I'm having some trouble with the last barrel, though. We keep bumping it." She rubbed at her sore knee. Tomorrow she'd definitely be bruised.

Bent's eyes narrowed in concern. "Your knees taking a beating, huh? We'll work on that soon."

"Okay." She pulled a bit of alfalfa from a bale and chewed on it. Silence stretched between them, a silence thick with unspoken messages, with nervous energy. Kate hadn't the least idea how to handle it, or how to handle Bent himself.

Suddenly she wearied of the game. Not looking at him, she took the hay from her mouth and studied it, as if it contained the answer to her question. "Bent," she whispered, "what do you *really* want here?"

The cowboy moved closer, so that his sturdy chest and thick arms came into her lowered vision. Revealed by rolled-up sleeves, his forearms were lined by raised veins and corded with muscle. His scent teased her, a combination of hay and horses and of something elusive she guessed to be his own unique skin fragrance. The man was very masculine, Kate thought. And very, very dangerous.

When he came to stop within inches of her and leaned one shoulder against the barn door, she swallowed her alarm. His reply was as soft as her query had been. "Don't you know what I want, Kate?"

Feeling caught in a trap that began with her own curiosity and ended with Bent's overwhelming presence, Kate found she couldn't move, could only raise her gaze to collide with his. He was staring at her, his expression taut with messages she didn't want to receive, was afraid to receive.

"I'll tell you why I'm really here, Kate," he surprised her by saying. "And you'd better listen." He turned toward the horse, releasing her gaze. She let out a pent-up breath she hadn't realized she'd been holding.

"I'm listening."

"I came today," he began, "to see for myself if you were overworking your mare. Obviously I was right."

"What do you mean *overworking*," She could only bluster. She hadn't expected *this*.

"You rode hard just yesterday, Kate. In the rodeo, remember? And first thing this morning you're working her again. She's not a four-year-old, she's getting on. Sierra needs rest. As of today, you're off her for two weeks."

"Two weeks!"

"No riding, no barrel racing. Lounging only. Got it?"

"B-but we've got to practice, improve our times. I can't lay off now, not with all those rodeos coming up!'' She lifted her chin and a new silence thickened, a silence of warring wills.

Bent crossed his arms. ''The quarter crack in her right front isn't bad, but with the pounding the circuit requires, it'll probably get worse. Now, the real season doesn't start for three weeks. You'll lay off for two, then start her back slow.'' His narrowed eyes dared her to argue.

She glared back, resenting him for pulling rank. She realized her teeth were gritted, her hands balled. But he *was* the trainer. With an effort, she pushed past her resentment enough to get out, ''Whatever you say, Murray.''

''Coffee cake's ready,'' came Mimi's soft bellow, and the spell was broken. But Kate wasn't fooled. She would face many more tests of will, as well as sexually charged moments with this man, before they were through.

Walking outside, they found Flash carrying a delicious-looking bundt cake, steaming hot and studded with pecans and a brown sugar topping. Behind him Mimi held a tray containing a coffeepot, four mugs, a cow-shaped creamer and sugar bowl.

Bent reached out. ''Let me take that,'' he said, lifting the tray from the older woman and putting it on a scarred picnic table next to the barn where Kate often ate lunch. ''Are you sure there's enough for me? Sunday mornin's my mama used to make fine-looking cakes such as this.'' He threw Mimi a beguiling smile—the type Kate had seen little boys use to charm cookies out of their grandmas.

''Of course there's enough,'' Mimi answered quickly, and she began fussing over the coffeepot. ''I'm glad you stopped by, young man. Kate's told me about you—and what a wonderful trainer you are, too! It's good news you'll be helping her.''

Kate felt her brows rise. She hardly ever saw even-keeled Mimi flustered. But she was acting like a schoolgirl being flirted with! And Flash had started firing questions at Murray about his old rodeo days and horse care and apparently anything that came into his young head. Not that Murray answered in much more than monosyllables. But Kate could see that he'd impressed both Flash and Mimi. *Damn cowboy,* she thought in irritation. She wished he'd just do his job and leave her loved ones alone.

He half sat on the edge of the table, his strong teeth sinking into the cake with such unabashed delight she could hardly hold on to her irritation. She guessed a single man like Murray rarely got home-baked goods.

"More coffee?" Mimi asked, holding up the pot.

Bent eagerly held out his mug. "Yes, ma'am. You do make a fine pot. Best I've had all year. Do you grind your own beans?"

"Good heavens, no." Mimi put a hand on her chest. "It's just store-bought."

"I'd never know." His tone was grave with respect and Kate rolled her eyes. *Grind your own beans, indeed!*

"*I* haven't had a cup yet," she put in, but no one heard her. She was forced to pour her own—and got the dregs of the pot, to boot.

When fifteen minutes had passed and Bent had completely ingratiated himself with Mimi, he slowly rose from the table and lazily stretched. "Guess I'll be on my way," he told the group at large. Naturally Mimi and Flash tried to get him to stay for lunch, but Kate said nothing at all, her silence conspicuous. He tilted his head as if considering the offer to stay, and Kate wondered if he was doing it to needle her. After a moment he declined. "Got to get back to the ranch."

"Yes," Kate raised her voice over the others' objections. "I'm sure you've got a lot to do. Goodbye."

Grinning, he took Mimi's blue-veined hand between his tanned palms and thanked her. Then he clasped Flash's hand and shook it so firmly the youth swayed. Kate could plainly see Flash's pleasure in being treated like a man grown.

Bent didn't touch Kate, instead tipping his hat and reminding her of their "date" at the coming rodeo.

"You mean our date to train," she qualified carefully, not liking his wording.

"Of course, Katie girl. What else?" He sauntered off toward the front of the house, where he'd left his truck, and Kate slumped against the barn door, folding her arms.

So he wanted her to let Sierra rest, did he? Then why hadn't he said so yesterday? Why drive three hours when a phone call would suffice?

More likely this trip was for looking over the merchandise, she thought darkly. He figured she was all bought and paid for, did he? Well, he was wrong.

Almost automatically she shied away from thinking about the night of passion he was evidently still expecting. The World was a long way off, and anything could happen. Her horse could become injured. Bent himself might quit. An earthquake might shake California into the sea.

Emerging from behind the house, Bent's white truck threw up a dust cloud and rumbled down the country lane. Kate watched him go with a baleful eye. She'd been wary of him before, but wary wasn't enough.

Now she was going on full alert!

Chapter Three

Bent stood at one end of the deserted arena, his booted feet spread wide, gray cowboy hat pulled low over his tanned face. Mounted on Sierra mere feet away, Kate found her gaze drawn to him time and again.

There was something special about this man, she mused in wonder, an element beyond his reputation as a world champion, beyond his blatantly masculine body and his hard, direct gaze.

She had no idea what that element might be, and no patience in herself to puzzle it out. Releasing a quick, restless breath, she shook off the odd notion and forced herself to concentrate.

In one hand Bent held a clipboard and in his other, a large stopwatch. This was their first formal training session and Kate was keyed up, thrilled to truly be Benton Murray's student. That was all it was, of course, she assured herself—the fact that the former star and champion was now her teacher. It explained her silly shortness of breath and accelerated pulse rate when their gazes met and locked.

The Redbluff Rodeo in California was over and he'd secured permission to use the empty arena. Only the bucking animals and roping steers were left as the stock contractor was scheduled to load them into his trailers early the next morning. Huge Brahman bulls, raw-boned bucking horses, and smaller, horned roping steers were crowded in the pens. A few dozed, tails swishing away flies in the late afternoon sunlight. Occasionally a steer would bawl and mill. A spotted gelding found room to lie down, its long hoofed legs tucked under it.

After the loud crush of the crowd and the blare of the announcer's loudspeaker, it seemed unnaturally quiet. Up in the stands, Sarah sat alone, avidly watching.

"Go ahead and take a few practice runs," Bent was saying. "I'll time you, watch your technique." He moved away and waited for Kate to make her run.

Drawing a deep, nervous breath, Kate guided Sierra outside the open gate, well back from the starting line between the two cones Bent had set up. The mare side-stepped and tossed her head, sensing the race to come. Without thinking, Kate began whispering to the horse, as she always did, urging her to give her all, to run and turn on a dime and fly like the champion horse Kate knew she was, knew she would be.

Ready now, Kate loosened the reins an inch and kicked the mare with the blunt rowels of her old spurs. Sierra made the first jump in a lunge, then raced for the righthand barrel. Kate reined the horse around it sharply and made for the second barrel, another tight tuck, and headed for the last one.

At the final turn, the mare slowed almost imperceptibly, but Kate urged her into full speed to the finish line. Coming to a sliding stop that sent up low clouds of soft dirt, Kate glanced at Bent.

He was staring down at the stopwatch. "Good," he pronounced. "But I noticed your mare slowing at the top of the triangle. Costs time. What's that about?"

"I don't know," Kate said, panting a little with the exertion. "She doesn't do it at home, but in the competition here yesterday she did it again. I think that was why we only came in third. Actually, she does it a lot away from home. And it's always at the last barrel."

Bent frowned. "I'll go over there—" he pointed with the clipboard to a spot close to where Sierra slowed "—and see if I can figure a reason."

Kate put the mare through the run three more times, and Bent watched closely. When she came to a stop and trotted back to Bent, he was already striding toward her. "It's the stock pens," he concluded. "She's getting distracted by the bucking animals. That's why she doesn't do it at home."

"Oh" was all Kate could say. Of course. Why hadn't she realized it?

"The key to a good barrel horse is speed, durability and heart. We know she's got speed—she runs like a four-footed whirlwind."

Kate smiled with pride and patted the sleek neck.

"She hauls well, and despite her hoof problems, she's shown that with care, she's durable," Bent went on. "The last ingredient is heart, and it's obvious to me she's full of it."

Feeling her smile broaden, Kate knew a surging joy. Benton Murray thought they were good enough!

"You, however," he began sternly, dashing her spirits, "need work."

"I do?"

"You ride well, and you're a team with your mare...but you're not aggressive enough." The contrary man had the nerve to smile at her after delivering the bombshell.

Kate swallowed her disappointment. "What should I be doing?"

"You're too upright in the saddle. Get your shoulders forward more—hold on to the horn when you round the barrels and keep your center of balance vertical. You're leaning with the horse, which is wrong."

She bit her lip. "So I *do* lean."

"Work on it," he ordered. "As for the stock animals—we'll just have to get Sierra used to them so she ignores them when she rounds the last barrel. After every rodeo, take her and tie her to the pen rails for an hour or so. She'll be able to look until she's bored. That's what we want—for her to think there's nothing interesting down there and so she'll keep her mind on business."

Nodding, Kate made careful mental notes. Despite his demanding tone, she tamped down her flare of resentment and vowed to listen and act on every point he taught her about the sport.

"We'll stop now," Bent decreed.

"But we've just begun," she cried. "I usually practice hours!"

"Exactly why we'll give your mare a rest now. As I said before, you're in danger of overworking her. Race her too much, and she's gonna come up lame, remember?''

For an instant she bristled, then realized she was being unreasonable. Chagrined, she murmured agreement. She dismounted and watched Bent stride away. Sarah came down from the bleachers and lingered behind. Kate couldn't help noticing that the girl had absorbed every word of Bent's lesson from the stands.

At the gate, Bent paused to call out precise instructions for Sierra's cooling and rubbing down, and Kate waited for his back to turn before she stuck her tongue out at him. The man was a brilliant trainer, but terribly arrogant, even autocratic. As if she didn't know how to care for Sierra! Seeing Kate's immature gesture, Sarah giggled.

"Will you help with my horse?" Kate asked, smiling.

Sarah laid a hand on the mare's neck. "She's sure fast."

"The fastest," Kate replied with pride. She glanced at the girl shrewdly. "You ever think about barrel racing?"

Sarah's eyes lit but she threw a nervous glance over her shoulder. "My dad won't let me. He says it's dangerous, that sooner or later, I could get hurt." A flash of rebellion appeared in her brown eyes. "But *he* rodeoed for years—riding the roughstock, no less."

They walked together to cool the horse, eventually leading her to the cross-ties. "Horses are big, strong, sometimes unpredictable animals," Kate allowed. "They can hurt a person without even trying, or meaning to—"

"That's what Dad says," Sarah muttered.

"But, for someone who's properly trained, the risks lessen. I'll bet you've spent your whole life around horses."

"Oh, I have," she agreed. "At Dad's home in Bakersfield I have a terrific gelding—Jake. But he's real old, twenty-four now, and he's not a barrel horse. Some day..."

Together they cared for Sierra, who accepted their ministrations calmly, batting at Kate with her soft nose until she took a moment to scratch the base of the mare's ears. Kate unsaddled her and Sarah took off her leg wraps. After a hose bath, they shampooed Sierra's mane and tail until the coarse hair shone black and full.

From her trailer, Kate got out a bag of sliced watermelon—Sierra's favorite treat—and enjoyed Sarah's laughter as the horse eagerly crunched the rind. "You know," Kate began slowly, feeling her way, "I think your dad is maybe a tad overprotective of you."

"No kidding." Sarah gave an unladylike snort.

"You're his only daughter, and he loves you. He doesn't want anything to happen to you. But...maybe he also doesn't realize that you're not a baby anymore."

"Sometimes he still treats me like a little kid." Sarah frowned and Kate knew she was on the right track.

"That's silly. Anybody can see you're growing into a young woman. Why, pretty soon you'll be a teenager!"

"Yeah."

Smiling to herself, Kate remembered chafing at her grandmother's strict ideas about raising her. Sarah began making small braids of Sierra's still damp mane, her delicate brows knit in concentration, and Kate's smile widened. Sarah was a nice kid. Well, she'd made a start with Bent's daughter, a good start. And he was holding up his end of the bargain. Perhaps, just perhaps, she really would have a shot at the title.

By midnight Kate had bedded down in the front of her horse trailer. Sleeping there saved motel costs; she had to conserve every penny, and it kept her close to Sierra. Morning found her up and in the arena bathroom. Since no one else was around so early, she made do with a thorough sponge bath and shampooed her hair in the sink. After dressing, she gathered her belongings. She was still towel-drying her hair when she heard a quiet sniffling.

Following the sound, she rounded the corner to discover Sarah slumped behind the bleachers, her back to a block wall. The girl wore her habitual too-big jeans. Morning sun shone chestnut highlights in her dark hair, but it straggled, unkempt, over her forehead. Seeing Kate, Sarah quickly averted her face and wiped surreptitiously at her eyes.

"Sarah, what's wrong?" Kate demanded, rushing over. "Are you all right?"

Sarah nodded, head still down.

"Is it your father?" she cried. "Is something wrong with Bent?"

Sarah shook her head vigorously. She hiccuped and took several deep breaths. "He's okay. It's... personal."

Sinking to the ground beside her, Kate let out a breath. "Ah." She set down her bag of clothing and continued to dry her hair. "Want to talk about it?"

"No. Thank you," she added, remembering her manners.

"All right. Well, just remember, if you need to talk with somebody, I have time." When Sarah nodded, Kate began to rise, then, unwilling to give up just yet, she sank back down. Feeling her way, she started to speak carefully. "Twelve is a hard age. I remember, believe me. I was in sixth grade, and I liked Tommy Woodward. He had the neatest hair, kinda long and blond, like a surfer. And he had a great German shepherd dog. But Tommy didn't like me. He was forever mooning over Miranda Farmer." Kate studied her nails. "He could have had me for a girlfriend, but he wanted Miranda, who scorned him. I really hated her."

Chancing a peep at Sarah, Kate studied her face. No change. So it wasn't boy trouble. She frowned, trying to figure out what else could be such a disaster in a twelve-year-old's life. "My grandmother raised me. I didn't have a mother, and my dad died when I was fourteen. Grandma sure was strict."

"I live with my grandma," Sarah offered. "She's real strict, too. But I love her. She's pretty cool."

So it wasn't her father or grandmother—parental problems. Kate rested her chin on her palm, running out of ideas. "How do you like school?" she tried. "Are you looking forward to eighth grade?"

Sarah looked up, startled, then her face crumpled and she wailed, "No!"

Bingo.

"Are your grades okay? Do you have a lot of friends?"

"That's just it. I got up this morning and realized that it's almost Easter and that..."

"That..." Kate leaned forward.

"Well, it'll be summer and then, uh, eighth grade. My friends all have moms. I don't. I just have

Grandma, and she has to rest a lot. My friend's moms take them shopping and, uh, help them with stuff.''

"Back-to-school shopping?" Kate hazarded. *That's* what this was about?

"Sort of," Sarah hedged. "It's more . . . what goes under the clothes." She shot a glance upward at Kate's face, then blushed furiously.

Suddenly Kate saw the light. "Sarah, do you need a bra?"

The girl gave a minuscule nod. "I *can't* ask my dad to take me. It'd be too embarrassing. All my friends have them. I just can't go to eighth grade without one."

"Of course not." Kate patted Sarah's knee and felt her heart warm. "I didn't get my first bra until I was in ninth grade."

"*No,*" Sarah breathed, horrified.

"Like with you, my grandma didn't notice, and I was too shy to say anything. So, for a whole year I wore baggy shirts that were too big for me. I suppose some grandmas are real observant, but ours aren't, huh?"

For the first time, Sarah smiled, showing her braces. Kate smiled back and felt a tenuous connection with her. How well she knew the loneliness of watching her friends with intact families going together on outings, back-to-school night, Disneyland. Kate loved Mimi, fiercely so. But it wasn't the same as having a mother.

Her father, when he'd been alive, was always quick to criticize, always difficult to please. His devastating pronouncement when she was thirteen still echoed in her head. *You want to barrel race? You wouldn't make it. You don't have what it takes.* Kate swallowed hard and thrust down the awful memory. Mimi believed in her. Mimi had been the one to insist Kate take the nest egg the older woman had been saving for years and go for a shot at the title.

"Don't worry about it," she told Sarah now. "I'll help you. We'll head over to the department store this morning. That way I'll be able to leave in the afternoon for the next rodeo."

They got to their feet and Sarah dug into the dirt with her high-topped tennis shoe. "Are you sure?"

"I'm going to the mall, anyway, to get some things for myself," she improvised quickly, careful of the girl's fragile pride. "It's no bother. Besides, you've helped me with Sierra. I owe you."

Kate found Bent adding oil to his truck engine and talking with a few last stragglers as they loaded their horses to leave town. The sleeves of his blue chambray shirt were rolled up to the elbows and revealed strong, tanned forearms. Set on the back of his head, a battered summer-weight straw hat allowed his dark hair to escape onto his forehead. A loose curl looking artfully arranged hung over his handsome face, though Kate knew the man probably never gave a thought to his hair except when it came time for a cut.

He looked up from the engine and caught her gaze. Each time she saw him, she felt the impact of his presence down to her toes. What was it about this particular man that made her jumpy...shivery?

She and Sarah walked up and Kate unceremoniously put out her hand. "We need some money, Bent. Sarah and I are going to the mall."

He straightened and wiped oil from his hands. "I'm getting ready to leave, Sarah," he said. "What do you need at the mall?"

The girl was silent, her eyes beseeching Kate, who instantly answered for her. "You have a daughter, cowboy, remember? A female? She needs some feminine things. I'm going to help her pick them out. You can leave in a couple of hours. Cash, please?" She wagged her fingers.

Looking puzzled, Bent glanced again at his daughter, who waited expectantly. He shrugged and dug into his wallet for several twenties. "All right," he grumbled. "But you'll be back by noon?"

"Two," Kate corrected, taking Sarah's hand and pulling her along behind. At Bent's deepening frown, Sarah giggled and she and Kate ran off like conspiratorial teenagers.

So that Kate wouldn't have to unhitch her truck from the trailer, they took the bus to the mall. At a large department store they decided on cotton bras and also chose two pair of fitted jeans and three tops, all in Sarah's true size. After a chili dog lunch, they bought ice cream scoops in waffle cones.

"You like my dad, huh?" Sarah's question sounded more like a statement, one filled with preadolescent slyness.

Instantly Kate grew wary. "He's okay," she answered, tasting her pistachio cone. "He's an excellent trainer."

She didn't like Sarah's knowing smile, but tried to shrug it off. Lord save her from intuitive young girls! "I think it's time we got back."

"He likes you, too," she said as if she hadn't noticed Kate's attempt to dismiss the subject. "He hasn't wanted to train anybody since I was born." Tilting her head, she gave Kate another sidelong glance. "You're special, though, aren't you?"

"Mimi says so," Kate answered lightly. She certainly wasn't going to let a smart twelve-year-old get her goat. Or the upper hand.

Back at the parking lot, Bent waited for them at his truck. Now nearly deserted, the rodeo grounds looked bare, save for the cleanup crew. When Sarah ran off to the bathroom to put on her new clothing, he hitched himself up onto his pickup's open tailgate. "Thanks," he said gruffly. "Guess it's been hard on Sarah, not having a mother and all. Her grandma and I do what we can by her."

"I know, Bent." Without thinking, Kate responded to the awkwardness and sensitivity in Bent's voice and laid her hand reassuringly on his arm. Her fingers curled around his muscular wrist. It was a gesture she would make for a friend who was hurting, nothing more, she assured herself. "Sarah's a wonderful girl—and you've done a good job."

At her touch, a sudden light flared in Bent's eyes. Kate withdrew her hand, her guard immediately rising. She had the unsettling image of an unlit fuse of dynamite and a candle flame coming too close together.

To distract him, she asked about Sarah.

Surprising her, he appeared to open up. "Sarah's mother was killed in an airplane crash in the desert. Some kind of engine failure. Sarah was staying with some of Alicia's friends at the time, and she was only about six months old. You might as well know that Alicia had left me long before she even had the baby. After she was born, Alicia wouldn't let me see her much."

"Oh, Bent," Kate sighed, feeling the heartbreak it must have cost him. She had to suppress the urge to reach out and clasp his arm again.

"Anyway..." His voice was rough and hesitant now, as if he had to force the words out. "I wasn't even sure Sarah was mine."

Kate gasped.

"I'm still not."

For the life of her, Kate had no idea what to say. His voice was flat, unemotional, when it should have been strained. His very lack of inflection caught at her—revealed more than he probably knew. The scars on Bent's heart had clawed deep, the wounds festering, lasting.

He was frowning heavily now, a scowl darkening his face. "When they brought me the baby, saying I was the only one left, I looked into those trusting brown eyes. In about two minutes I didn't care anymore. She was mine for good."

Yards away, another pickup's motor roared to life and pulled out. The driver waved goodbye. There was only one other truck left in the packed-dirt parking lot—an older roper still grooming his horse. Kate barely noticed.

"You formed a bond," she concluded slowly, "which had nothing to do with blood ties, and everything to do with love."

The cowboy looked away. "I guess."

"She lives with your mother, though," Kate noted carefully. "Why not you?"

He lifted one big shoulder. "I'm gone a lot—shoeing. Someday Sarah will be with me all the time, when I get enough to buy the spread I want."

"You want to buy a ranch?" Kate asked, thinking. There were still wide open and beautiful ranch lands available in California. It was something she'd wanted her entire life.

Bent scowled, looking into Kate's wide eyes. Had he said too much? It wasn't like him, running off at the mouth like that. His only excuse had to be Kate's warm curiosity, her sweet compassion. Against his will, he realized he could get used to it. She made him feel comfortable, like a man ought to feel around a warm, interested woman.

In the past bleak years he'd been completely bereft of a woman's softer side. Oh, there had been women here and there. Some he'd met in a bar, bought a drink, and gone home with, if only for an hour or two. Nothing beyond such shallowness had developed. He hadn't allowed it.

Kate Monahan, though, could reach beyond his defenses and draw the emptiness from his soul.

There was danger in such thinking.

She touched him often; he wondered if she realized how much. Earlier in the day he'd found himself looking for her, wishing she would return from the damn shopping mall with Sarah and lay her small hand on his arm, as she was wont to do.

Now, as he continued looking into her expressive hazel eyes, thoughts crept in, thoughts of hands sliding on bodies. Warm, bare bodies. Naturally such ideas progressed to strobelike images of agonizingly slow, intensely satisfying sex. He had no trouble at all imagining Kate smiling beneath him, nothing covering her but the few freckles that cascaded over her nose...and himself.

At his continued silence, she blushed, and he supposed she could read his expression, divine what was going on in his mind. He lifted his hand to toy with a strand of her blond hair that had escaped her braid.

Her lips were a soft pink, softly parted in a way that he bet would turn a pious monk into an amorous fiend. With the pad of his thumb, he tested her mouth's velvety texture. She went perfectly still, and Bent was inordinately pleased to hear a low catch in her breath. The dark pupils in her hazel-green eyes expanded—a physical reaction to his touch. Inside he felt a surge of male satisfaction. No matter what she said, he knew she was as attracted to him as he was to her.

Without thinking and completely on impulse, he wondered aloud if she would like to pay her debt to him now.

Beneath his hand he felt her stiffen as she went ramrod straight. Instantly he knew his mistake.

"What debt?" she challenged. "I didn't go for your sordid deal, remember? I'm paying you money from my winnings and giving help with Sarah. That's *all*." She wrenched away.

Hell, he'd gone about that wrong. Had it been so long since he'd wooed a woman that he'd forgotten all the subtleties, the protocol?

He never knew what devil made him grab her arm. Misplaced male ego? Wounded pride? He heard his own words, rasped out roughly. "I know I'm too old for you, Kate, but you're a grown woman. Maybe you didn't say yes with words, but your eyes told me plain enough. I *will* collect what's due me."

Anger and outrage tightened Kate's face and he felt more the heel than ever. He did truly admire her ambition. Yet at the same time, he feared it.

"You'll get what's due you when you go to hell, where you belong." She flipped her braid over her shoulder, glaring at him.

He smiled without mirth. "Most likely."

"Furthermore, don't for a second think you can push me into bed. It's not going to happen." With that she swept away from him, going to load up her horse.

He watched with a mixture of mounting frustration and half-suppressed guilt. As he hooked his thumbs into the front pockets of his jeans, the devil prodded him again. "Don't worry, honey," he told her, "when we go to bed, it'll be because you want it as much as me."

Without further acknowledgment, Kate closed the rear gates and slammed herself into the cab.

Not far off, the old roper grooming his horse prepared to leave. He was well-liked on the circuit and both Kate and Bent knew him.

Now he called out, "Hey, Murray, heard you're training young Kate there." He smiled, teasing. "Thought you'd given up that sissy stuff years ago."

Bent glowered at the man, grumbling, "Must have lost my mind, agreeing to it." His gaze swung back to Kate and saw her smug smile. She enjoyed watching him squirm, he could see that.

Setting her truck in drive, she roared off, leaving him choking on the rising dust.

Despite his casual act, regret and dust were bitter in his mouth.

Alicia had had such ambition. Not as a competitor, but, he'd discovered too late, as a gold digger. She'd wanted a man who was a winner, not a loser, and loyalty had never been her strong suit. The ambition in Alicia, though different, bore uncomfortable resemblance to the ambition in Kate. Both women would do whatever it took to win; they would succeed at all costs.

Hell, it was probably for the best he'd scared Kate off. They wouldn't work—him, a man long frozen inside with nothing to offer a good woman. And her, an aspiring rider on her way to glory and fame. He was too old for her...too old. Their worlds would only connect for this brief time and would then spin apart.

And he must never allow himself to forget the most important factor in the equation: he really couldn't trust Kate any more than he could ever trust Alicia.

Chapter Four

Three short weeks sped past. Kate carefully recalled Bent's instructions each time she competed, and she and Sierra performed well. The Mother Lode Roundup Rodeo crowd at Sonora, California, was loud, excited, and their excitement communicated to Kate. Just as she was being called by the rodeo announcer to ride, Bent appeared at the chutes. In the three-week interim, she'd thought of him often—too often.

Still, by the end of the twenty-one days she'd convinced herself that her attraction to him would prove a passing thing. He was arrogant and egotistical and at times overbearing. Handsome as sin, though, and she appreciated handsome men. That was all it was.

As she held a tight rein on Sierra and spied Bent standing at the arena rails, he met her gaze and lifted his hat, then gave her the thumbs-up. She knew in an instant she'd fooled herself.

She drew a deep, deep breath. Was the pounding of her heart induced by his appearance or the adrenaline of the coming run? She wasn't sure which. As always, Sierra was closely attuned to her moods, and the mare worried the bit, her sides quivering, nostrils flaring.

They were off.

They flew around the course.

They won.

Behind the chutes a mere minute later, Bent approached with a wide smile and grasped Sierra's bridle. Kate beamed down at him.

"You *are* good," he declared. "Real good."

Laughing with joy, she inclined her upper body toward him. "We're okay, huh?"

"The best."

Reaching up, he settled his hands at her waist and half pulled her from the saddle. She let him take her weight. When her feet were on the ground, he crushed her briefly to his chest.

He could tell by her surprised expression that she hadn't expected the gesture. Truthfully, he was just as surprised as she was.

"Great run, honey." Reluctantly he let his hands fall away from her. Her eyes sparkled, her smile was wide and welcoming. The back of her wine-hued shirt was damp and her skin emanated a mixture of soapy freshness and clean perspiration. He found the combination incredibly arousing. Staring at her, he admitted something to himself: he'd missed her. "Congratulations."

"Thank you," she breathed. "I didn't lean, did I?"

"Nope."

"I've been tying Sierra close to the stock pens after every rodeo and I think she's getting used to the animals." Her words tumbled out and he easily read her eagerness to please him. "You were absolutely right about her being distracted by them." Tilting her head upward to look into his face, Kate appeared innocent and young. Eager. For the life of him, he couldn't take his eyes off her.

In another second he'd be rock hard.

For long moments Kate found herself staring into Bent's tanned features, the three weeks falling away. It was wonderful to win with him watching her, supporting her. His praise made her flush with new confidence and boundless energy. Why, she wanted to go right back out and make the run again and again.

Suddenly Kate had new insight into her own motivations. Beyond her desire to win for Mimi, beyond her wish to banish the shadows of her father's lack of faith, a new goal presented itself: she wanted to make Bent proud.

As the afternoon waned, Bent picked up two shoeing jobs. Many of the old-timers on the circuit remembered him and knew how adept a farrier he'd become. Kate had cooled Sierra, given her a little water and a carefully measured mixture of oats, corn, hay and bran, then stabled her in a set of temporary stalls.

The heat of the day was relieved by a new breeze, leaving only a pleasant warmth. As the sun dropped, dust motes chased each other in the last beams of golden light slanting tiger stripes through the bleachers. Kate reclined on some spread out hay near the shoer's rack, watching Bent do his work. She could afford to relax tonight.

In the cross-ties, a heavily muscled palomino moved restlessly, and Bent spoke to it in low tones. Behind him was his truck, which resembled a mobile machine shop with a bewildering array of tools. In addition to a forge and anvil, there was a welder, a band saw, hand tools and a drill press.

Sarah perched on the tailgate, asking questions and observing as Bent explained the procedure for rasping a hoof.

"Can I try it, Dad?" Sarah asked shyly.

Kate could see his surprise. "Sure, honey." Letting down the hoof, he made room for Sarah. She lifted the palomino's right hind foot and began an awkward rasping. She had none of Bent's rhythmic competence or sureness of movement, and Kate found herself watching Bent's reaction closely. Her own father would have quickly elbowed her away, waving her off to let him "do the job right."

Bent, however, only offered encouragement and a few pointers.

"Can I nail the shoe on?" Sarah asked.

He nodded. "I've trimmed the sole and the frog. Now we'll use the hoof nippers and then fit the shoes to the horse. Here's some nails. I keep 'em in my mouth for my daily dose of iron." From his bent-over position, he grinned at his daughter and she smiled back. Kate smiled, too. Though sometimes abrupt and demanding with Kate herself, Bent was unfailingly kind and gentle with Sarah. In moments of doubt, this facet of his personality reassured Kate. Any man so loving to his daughter must have potential.

Kate watched in wonder and a sort of lonely regret. If only her father had had such patience with her. If only he'd been as kind, as attentive.

"When I die," she said to Bent impulsively, "I want to come back as your daughter."

Bent straightened, his hand going, as always, to rub his lower back. He took a nail from his mouth and grinned at her. "I, for one, am glad we're not related. I'm glad you're a woman...and I'm a man."

A quickly smothered titter came from Sarah's direction, though she kept her face averted and her hands busy.

In a wonderful mood after her win and the pleasantness of the day, Kate decided to let his comment pass. She only smiled and said nothing. When Bent leaned down again to teach Sarah, Kate realized she found intense enjoyment in observing him perform his work. She liked seeing his corded arms flex as he hammered nails into hooves, liked watching his thigh muscles contract when he bent low.

It would be so easy to want his company forever.

Around him life became fascinating, and when he wasn't there, she wished he was. In his presence her body often felt fever heated, her every sense on alert. Sitting up, Kate wrapped her arms around her knees and picked bits of straw from her jeans.

Sometimes lately it felt as if her thoughts were running away from her. A vague bell of alarm sounded somewhere in her psyche, but the source seemed elusive.

Bent was her trainer, nothing more. Though today he seemed at ease, she still often sensed in him a deep unhappiness. She'd learned that he was normally very quiet, to the point of being withdrawn. Among the rodeo competitors he had friends, but he had little to do with women. Kate liked that about him.

Just so she didn't find *too* many things to like.

Kate frowned. It wouldn't do to give Bent the power of her affection. No one knew better than she that his heart was frozen.

He would use a woman. But he would never love her.

Three more weeks passed. Then three more. Bent appeared at fairly regular intervals for training sessions. He had much to teach her, and eager student that she was, she soaked up his tutoring like a dry sponge.

Now, after the first performance of the Sisters Rodeo in Oregon, she passed the time with Flash Johnson, who'd finished, as usual, out of the calf-roping money. In fact, he'd finished dead last. Flash sometimes went "down the road" with her, exchanging the ride for gas money, and Kate enjoyed his unflagging optimism. He always felt that he would do better in the next town, and privately Kate hoped so, or he would soon run out of his small savings.

The evening had been slow, and though it was growing dark, Kate wasn't tired. Flash, with a rope always in his hands or nearby, began performing the roping tricks he was forever practicing. Whirling a huge loop overhead, he kept it turning, then lowered it to step through.

One leg made it through the hole, the other didn't, and the rope tangled around him like a child's jump rope. Kate laughed and Flash grinned sheepishly. "I'll get it," he promised. "Just give me a minute to work it out."

On the straw bale where she sat, someone dropped his weight beside her. When she turned, her breath caught. Bent wasn't due to meet her for another week, so she hadn't been expecting him. He slouched back against the barn, resting his weight on his spine, and hooked one booted foot onto his opposite knee. "Howdy, ma'am," he drawled, and Kate smiled.

She pretended to tip an imaginary hat. "Howdy, cowboy," she replied in a pronounced Western drawl. "You bring in the bulls from the south forty yet?"

He grinned and played the game. "A'course, Miz Monahan. And I branded all them late calves like you wanted. Supper ready?"

They both laughed while Flash looked on, completely baffled. When they didn't explain, he resumed practice.

Kate glanced at Bent. He was tanned and smiling— a fabulously handsome man with a cocksure tilt to his gray hat and an ever-present gleam in his amber eyes. For the life of her, she couldn't look away.

Fortunately, he was watching Flash. After a moment he rose and, without fanfare, asked for Flash's rope. With a dexterity beautiful to watch, Bent easily demonstrated a few fancy maneuvers. Flash ran to get another rope and tried to mimic him. But Kate could see that a rope came alive in Bent's hands—that he could do incredible things with it others could not.

Into her mind came the image of him on the first day they'd met, when he'd leapt onto a buckskin's back and raced off to expertly lasso the escaping Brahman bull.

Bent roped a nearby trash can and Flash followed suit, his own rope settling gently over Bent's. Soon the two men were in a friendly competition. Together they roped the sideview mirror of a steer wrestler's truck, a fire hydrant, and a very surprised, very unhappy passing dog.

While they removed the ropes and patted the dog, Kate laughed. She wasn't prepared for Bent's rope to come slithering out and snare her outstretched foot. At the home end, Bent gave a gentle tug, as if to pull her off the straw bale, and Kate raised a playful fist. "You'd better not, cowboy," she threatened.

"No?" He gave another playful tug. "What will you do?"

Kate sent him a mock glower. She enjoyed seeing him so lighthearted for a change. "I'll...tip over every barrel at the next rodeo, then I'll tell everyone that's how *you* trained me."

He laughed, a free-sounding, deep-throated laugh she liked. The devilish gleam came back into his eyes. "Is that the worst you can do? Don't you want to tie me up and torture me?"

She would *not* blush. "I'll tie you up, all right. And then dump you in the Willamette River."

"Hey, watch me," Flash called out, expertly roping a stool.

Another cowboy sauntered by, Barry Engan, a tall, broad-shouldered man with a handlebar mustache, who'd won the calf roping average that day. "You should hope to be so good catching the actual calves, Flash," he decreed. His words were teasing, but his tone had bite. Flash flushed to the roots of his hair. Kate frowned, knowing he was still smarting from his last-place finish.

"Funny," Kate called after the man, knowing an urge to defend her friend. "You're just scared of him. You know he'll beat your measly old four-second record someday."

Barry Engan's thick brows rose. "That measly time got me a state record, little lady. A little faster than your friend here. Why'd they call you Flash, anyhow, son? You'll be gone in a flash, maybe?"

Bent coiled his rope and his amber gaze chilled. "Butt out, Engan."

Suddenly, violent undercurrents crackled in the air. As the two men faced off, Kate's eyes widened and she held her breath. She had the fleeting impression that blows were about to be struck.

Engan took long moments to inspect Bent, one hand hanging on to the huge trophy buckle strapped over his stomach. "Sure, Horseshoer," he said to Bent casually, but Kate could hear the insult in his words. *From world champion rider down to horseshoer.* "See you around."

With that the man sauntered off the way he'd come, and Bent glared after him, eyes narrowed.

"You know him?" Flash asked in a low voice.

A muscle jumped in Bent's jaw as he threw the rope down. For long seconds Kate didn't think he'd answer. Finally he grumbled, "Yeah. I know him."

Seeing him so angry, Kate decided now was not the time to get to the bottom of the mystery. Nevertheless, she couldn't help wondering. The two had sounded like old enemies.

After a moment Flash stared down at the rope in his hands. "I've always believed that practice makes perfect. All I know is, I'm gonna keep practicing until I get better. I'm not gonna give up."

"Good," Bent said, and Kate nodded encouragement, but another thought nagged at her. His championship career had been founded on roughstock riding: bucking bulls and horses. But with a rope, Bent was obviously gifted. It wasn't unusual to find rodeo cowboys who had been raised on a ranch or farm and could use a rope. And to Kate's fairly knowledgeable eye, he was very good.

With effort she suppressed the urge to again demand why he didn't use this skill in the arena. After all, such skill was worth money—it could bring him closer to his dream of buying a ranch.

"Flash," she said carefully, "you like calf roping, but have you ever considered the team event? Maybe you'd like it better."

"Team roping?" When he looked at her blankly, she cut her eyes toward Bent.

Flash was nothing if not quick. "Uh, I guess I could try it. Maybe it'd be fun, having a partner." Pausing, he drew a breath of courage. Youthful hope shone in his eyes. "Bent, would you ever consider it? With somebody like me, I mean?"

In surprise and dismay Kate watched Bent's face darken. He shook his head. His voice was curt. "Thanks, no."

Lips firmed, Kate studied him narrowly. She really didn't think she could keep quiet much longer. As soon as she got him alone, she was going to get to the bottom of this.

They were alone much sooner than she'd guessed.

As dusk's fingers slowly pulled sunlight from the day, lamps began to cast pools of warm apricot light around the area. Flash was called away by two of his buddies, and when Kate looked around for Sarah, she couldn't find her. "She stayed home this trip," Bent explained. "She's decided to plant tomatoes and green beans in the yard with my mother."

"Vegetables, huh?" Kate said, wishing she had time to plant produce. Maybe someday. "I'll miss seeing Sarah, but I wanted a private word with you, anyway."

Predictably his heavy brows arched. "Then come into my office." He took her arm, guiding her past a knot of bull riders discussing a rank bull, and a few straggling spectators who'd managed to wrangle their way behind the scenes. Next to Bent's pickup sat a small living trailer.

Warily she thought about the tight, personal confines of his trailer, knowing that's where he would be sleeping. Her steps dragged when they neared the door. "Uh, it's such a warm evening. Let's talk out here."

He stopped and folded his arms, his gaze raking her cynically. "I'm not gonna jump you, Katie girl."

Her chin lifted. Always, he spoke plainly. She would return the favor. "Promise?"

"What do you think I am?" He snorted. "A monster?"

"No, just a man with a very strong—"

"Sex drive?" he finished for her.

"Libido," she corrected delicately.

"Same difference."

Summoning a sweet expression, she clasped her hands together. He would *not* be allowed to intimidate her. "I believe you have a couple of folding chairs on your truck somewhere? Shall we get them?"

He muttered something, but produced the chairs.

"So what is it?" he demanded when they were seated and he'd rummaged two colas from his trailer refrigerator.

She picked at the pop top of the can, wondering how to ease into the subject. "It's about helping young people," she ventured. "It's about encouraging them and giving of oneself for the good of others. Sharing knowledge. Teaching. Sacrificing."

Bent's expression of bewilderment was a thing of beauty, and if Kate hadn't been so serious she might have laughed. "What the hell are you talking about?" he demanded.

"I'm talking about Flash."

A beat of time passed. Roughly he took the cola from her hands, flipped open the can and thrust it back to her. "I'm not going to team rope with Flash Johnson, Kate. I told you before, I don't want anything to do with rodeo—beyond training you, that is."

"It would mean so much," she told him gravely. "He *needs* someone to take him under his wing. He's not without talent, and he's frantic to learn."

"None of my concern." He took a long swig of cola.

"Please consider it. You know I'm right. Think how thrilled he'd be if you would team up with him—why, that alone could give him the confidence he needs to improve and succeed." She was being pushy and she knew it. But this was so important.

Bent was stonily silent.

"Didn't anyone take you under his wing when you were a young, rookie rodeo rider? Didn't someone help you?"

When his eyes flickered, she knew she'd hit a nerve.

Bullheadedly, he fought her. "I'm trying not to get mad, Kate, so just drop it—"

Quickly she reached out, capturing his callused hand. "Don't get mad. I don't want you to be angry with me." Soothingly she cradled his hand between her two.

And just as quickly his anger evaporated. She watched his gaze lower to look at their clasped hands. Something in his eyes briefly gleamed. Then he gave a long sigh. "I used to be a good roper. On the ranch it was part of daily life. My father taught me, expected me to learn, and I did. But back then all I wanted was to ride the roughstock. Riding held all the excitement of a shouting crowd, thousands calling my name. And winning gave me glory. The buckles. The money. The attention. It was addictive. Maybe you don't understand."

"I do," she breathed, caught up in the picture he painted.

He studied her face. "Maybe you do, at that. Anyway... roping takes daily practice, work. I'm not even sure I can rope very well anymore."

"But you got that big Brahma with one loop!"

He shrugged. "Luck."

"Oh, luck, is it?" She smiled. "Then just carry your lucky rabbit's foot. That solves that problem."

He grinned at her, acknowledging that many rodeo contestants believed in lucky charms and in superstition. One saddle bronc rider she knew had a pair of lucky socks he refused to wash. Another cowboy recited the Lord's prayer exactly four times before each ride. There were others.

"You could practice," Kate suggested.

"Nah." His free hand clenched into a fist. "I don't want to make a fool of myself and maybe embarrass Flash in the process. I'd end up doing more harm than good."

The uncertainty in him caught Kate by surprise. She'd sensed all along that he was vulnerable beneath his prickly exterior. But now that he was sharing his vulnerability with her, it made her feel humble inside, and grateful. She was absolutely certain he didn't go around exchanging confidences with every barrel racer he met.

It was Bent's pain that made her give in to the urge to comfort him. What she hadn't known was that his need created a reciprocal need in herself. From deep inside her most feminine core, an urging to give to him was born. More than all the romancing in the world, more than all the earth-shattering kisses or avowals of affection, she discovered that a strong man's vulnerability could melt the hardest woman's heart.

"You can do it, Bent," she swore, clutching his hand. "I know. You're a champion, a winner. The ability to win is deep inside you. Okay, so maybe it's buried after all these years, but a person never loses such a talent."

He looked at her strangely. "You make it sound like anything's possible."

Saying nothing, she smiled.

In one smooth motion he got to his feet, drawing her with him. "Don't look at me like that, Katie girl. You make a man think of things best ignored." He stared at her hard, the gray light of dusk throwing his features into shadowed relief under the brim of his hat.

Building emotion swirled in her chest. The deep-seated female instinct to please a man, her admiration of Bent and his accomplishments, her growing attraction to him, all coalesced into a tight ball of need. She daren't hope he might kiss her. She tried not to look at his mouth.

He took a step closer, crowding her backward around the chair until her shoulder blades touched the side of his trailer. His hands were on her upper arms now, cupping them to curve down her back and draw her into his chest.

With no more warning than that, his mouth lowered swiftly and took hers with a tender fury she'd only dreamed about. His uniquely personal scent wrapped around her like sensual incense.

On her closed lips, his tongue gently probed until she opened for him. Quickly broaching this barrier, he sought the intimate, sensitive corners of her mouth.

Kate shivered, overwhelmed.

Kissing Bent was more thrilling than the most exhilarating ride. The ground sped past, spun around as if she were flying. Rushing wind, weightlessness, joy, she felt them all and, for once, decided to savor them all. What was one little kiss? What harm could there be? Caught up in the ever-deepening fog of sensual heat, she could think of no objections.

He was holding her so tightly she had to fight to free her arms, trapped between their bodies, to stand on tiptoe and coil them around his neck. Her breasts flattened on his hard chest, and when he shifted position, friction between them brought her nipples forth to sensitive peaks. For brief seconds Kate had to break contact with his mouth, gasping for air.

In the encroaching darkness, she saw the white flash of his teeth and felt the rumble of his chuckle against her breasts. Before she could utter a word, he was taking her mouth again. This time he used his tongue to tenderly stroke her lower lip. He made the pass once, then repeated it against her upper lip. At the cupid's bow of her mouth, he paused to sip from her skin.

Fire and lightning streaked to her very core.

He was tasting her.

At the edges of his collar where his dark hair brushed, she slipped her fingers through the silky strands, clasped the back of his tanned neck with her palm. Longing and desire mounted within her heart, caused her to arch into him closer yet.

Never still, his broad palms swept from her nape to below her belt line, where the top of her derriere curved down to the gentle flare of her hips. His hands were warm on her body, and Kate reveled in Bent's possessive touch, his caresses bringing intense enjoyment. Into her mind swirled erotic images of his hands palming her breasts, her belly, and lower.

Knees growing weaker by the moment, Kate knew wonder at her own reaction, and at the powerful attraction she felt for Bent. No other man had ever made her come so alive inside. No man but Benton Murray. Against his lips she breathed his name.

"Sweetheart," he rasped, "you're driving me crazy. Maybe you don't know much about men, so I'll tell you. You're encouraging me to think about things you say you don't want. Make up your mind."

He pulled back an inch, and in the deepening shadows she could hardly see his face, but she could see his eyes. They were burning with a deep amber fire.

He was right, and he was being incredibly gentlemanly to give her a chance to break the embrace, to send him away, reject him.

If she but had the will.

Through the sensual haze misting out common sense and rational thought—an elusive haze that clouded her senses and her mind—she wondered: was it so wrong to want a kiss?

She must have uttered the thought aloud, because he groaned, a low, guttural sound of masculine need and satisfaction. He was going to kiss her again.

"Hey, Murray," came a laughter-filled call from the older roper who'd teased him before. "You got that filly, Kate, in training, huh? Way to start 'em young." He guffawed at his own joke and ambled off. Kate blushed when she heard chuckles from the bull riders they'd passed earlier.

Bent jerked away, shocking her. Cool night air pooled down the front of her body, chilling her where seconds ago she'd been so very warm. Lifting his hat, he plowed stiff fingers through his hair. "He's right. You're just a baby." He glared at her accusingly.

Disbelief and hurt sliced through her sense of longing. An abrupt anger clawed at her. "But not too young to sleep with?" she retorted.

Again he ran an agitated hand through his hair, then resettled the hat. "I want you," he admitted starkly. "Until I remember how old I am next to you. There's fourteen years between us."

"Fourteen and a half," she corrected precisely, fingers shaking from reaction and pain.

"Yeah." His tone was sullen.

"Isn't it getting a little late to be worried about the age difference, Bent?" At her sides her arms hung straight and tense, her fingers clenched into tight fists against their sudden trembling. "If you recall, *you're* the one who wanted me to trade my body for your training. How would you feel if I'd taken you up on that?"

He shrugged and was silent.

"Guilty, that's how," she guessed, studying him shrewdly.

"Go on." His voice was rough, as if it pained him to speak. "Leave me alone."

She reached out to touch his arm, but he yanked it away. "Just get out of here, Katie *girl*." With an emphasis on the last word, he flung open his trailer door and slammed inside.

Chapter Five

Kate awoke in the makeshift bed she'd fashioned in her horse trailer to the blinding sunlight of morning and the rhythmic clang of hammer against anvil. An educated guess produced only one answer to the question of the noise: Bent was shoeing Sierra.

Groggily she rubbed her eyes and yawned. Bent probably thought he was going to fit Sierra's special shoes and then light out. Well, she had other plans for him.

Yawning again, she stretched. Eyes drifting closed, she relived the kiss they'd shared last evening in the half light of dusk. Sensual, passionate, fantastic. He'd ruined it all by his fierce rejection. She shifted on the bed and the memory burned.

When the day came for her to give herself to a man, she wanted it to be as a woman does for one she loves—with that love fully returned. *Not* as part of a business deal. Not solely because of shared lust. Recalling her abandoned response to him, Kate swallowed and decided to remind herself of this often. Bent was right to put her away, and she ought to be grateful to him, rather than hurt, even if she found his ideas about their age difference wrongheaded and irrelevant. In the meantime, they were bound in a business deal already spelled out.

She didn't like loose ends. She didn't like unhappy people around her. It had always been her nature to *do* something about problems that came her way, and she was certain that getting Bent to utilize his roping skills would make him a happier man. It would certainly make Flash happy to have such a partner.

After tidying up her flannel blankets on the straw, she slid into her jeans, boots, and a long-sleeved soft green shirt that emphasized the color of her eyes. Making do with a purse-size mirror, she swiped a quick bit of coral lipstick across her mouth. Hair in a braid, she jammed a lightweight Western straw hat on her head.

Opening the trailer door, she dropped to the ground and saw Bent was indeed shoeing Sierra, one of her front hooves held between his strong knees. Sunlight glittered over dew on the grass beneath her mare's hooves and shone a lustrous gleam on Sierra's glossy brown hide.

She noticed Bent watching her from her horse's side, a ballpeen hammer in his fist. "Mornin'," he said. Cautiously, it appeared to her.

Well, he should be wary, after his rejection of her the night before. Any other female would have booted him right into the next county. Or at least out of her life.

Coolly, she nodded to him, more determined than ever to bring him around. Still, it wouldn't hurt him to sweat awhile. "I hope you're not planning on leaving soon, because I'll be needing your services tonight."

With that enigmatic statement, she strode away, and it pleased her that his mouth was so full of nails he couldn't say a another word. It was just as well. She was on a mission.

She went in search of the stock contractor, finally finding the burly, white-haired man on the chute platform, where he was directing the men below about which bulls to put into which pens.

"Well, Kate, honey," Randolf Radden greeted her, hitching up the belt that was almost invisible beneath his enormous belly. "You come to your senses yet and decide to marry me?"

She batted her eyes at him and smiled coyly. It was an old game between them. "A girl needs time to make such an important decision, Randy. You'll have to let me think on it some more."

His eyes twinkled. "Sure. Thought I'd lost you is all. Heard that stud, Murray, was kissin' on you last night."

Her grin wavered. "It was just a kiss, that's all. Let's not make a big deal out of it." *Damn* it. Did everyone on the circuit know? She would have thought the bull riders would have more important things on their minds. "Anyway, I've a favor to ask." She plowed ahead, forcing her smile to widen. "Could you loan me a few roping steers for Bent and Flash to practice with tonight?"

"What?" The older man affected a horrified air. "And let those no-good, worthless ole boys sour my good steers? Why, I wouldn't trust those two farther'n I can throw an elephant against a strong wind."

She folded her hands and remembered the hungry force of Bent's kiss. Trust Bent? Grimly she smiled. "Neither would I. So, will you—loan us the steers?"

He leaned toward her, waggling his wiry white brows. "Not for anybody else, little lady. But since it's you askin' so sweetly, I s'pose I can loan you some stock."

Swiftly she reached up and pecked him on his heavy jowls. He chuckled, going back to his work, and she headed for the temporary stalls, looking for Ty Banning, the cowboy whose buckskin horse Bent had borrowed when he'd roped the escaping bull.

Since it was common among ropers to borrow a friend's horse in exchange for a percentage of any winnings, Kate had no reservations about asking Ty for the loan of his buckskin for some preliminary practice.

After obtaining permission for use of the arena and chutes that night some two hours after the last rodeo performance, she found Flash and told him her plans. He was thrilled.

"Bent's agreed to this?" he asked, hardly able to believe his good fortune.

"Why not?" she hedged. "It's only practice—to see if he likes it. If he can do it. You can heel, can't you?" The heeler was a member of the two-person team whose job it was to rope the steer's hind feet. This was done after the header caught the horns.

"Sure," he said enthusiastically. "Actually, that's what I've always been best at."

"Perfect." She frowned, thinking of the way Bent roped. "Because I'm sure Bent will be best at heading."

Since he was appearing at so many rodeos to train Kate, he was constantly picking up jobs. She noticed he never turned one down, which told her how anxious he was to earn every bit of money he could—probably to get the California ranch he'd said he wanted.

Now at a concrete-sided shoeing rack, he was rasping the enormous hoof of an ill-mannered black gelding. The June weather had him perspiring and dark rings had formed beneath his arms. Twin trickles of sweat trailed down his cheeks.

Kate came to a stop beside him. When the horse jerked his leg away for the third time, knocking the rasp from his hand, he swore softly, rubbing his bruised knuckle. She'd waited until late in the day to explain to Bent what she had arranged. The denial was not long in coming.

"No," he said adamantly, turning his back on her again to lift the gelding's big hoof and trap it firmly between his knees.

"Yes."

"No."

"Yes." She tugged at his shirt from behind. She could see she was going to have to use every weapon she had at her disposal, feminine wiles included. Drawing a breath, she plunged in. "You'll do it because you owe me."

He barked a short laugh, glancing up. "*Owe* you?"

"Certainly you do. Last night you took advantage of me. I…" Carefully she tried to assume the visage of an innocently wronged young girl. "I haven't much experience around men." Acting nervous and embarrassed, she stared down at her tightly twined hands. "No one's ever come on so strong before. The boys my age don't."

Peeking from beneath her lashes, she checked to see if he'd believe that "boys" her age would be as reticent as she was painting them. But she figured he viewed her as so young and immature that he just might have forgotten how *he'd* behaved at twenty-four.

As she'd hoped, his features took on an uneasy expression. He let the hoof down, set aside the rasp and straightened. Lifting his hat, he ran his fingers through his hair in a gesture she was quickly coming to associate with him. "Don't try that, Kate. I know plenty of men have come on to you. Besides, I feel guilty enough as it is—"

"Don't apologize," she cut in. "Just make it up to me this way. Rope with Flash tonight. Please? It's all set up."

Confusion was instantly replaced by hints of suspicion. "Why is it I get the feeling I'm being manipulated?"

"Can't imagine. So, will you do it?" She waited expectantly.

He half turned away, but she sensed his surrender. "Next you'll want a pound of flesh," he muttered, going around his truck to flip on the ear-splitting grinder, to end, she was sure, any more conversation. He caught up an iron shoe and shaped it in a shower of red sparks, but she didn't care. Let him grumble. He was going to rope.

At eleven o'clock that night, Kate ushered a grudging Bent to the arena and handed over reins to the already saddled buckskin. Overhead, the night's black sky was relieved only by a few flickering stars and the closer-in flood of arena lights.

Kate breathed in the clean air in satisfaction. It was a perfect night for roping. Why, someday, she might take it up herself.

At the buckskin's saddle horn, an excellent nylon-poly fiber rope lay neatly coiled. Bent went to the horse's head, stroked him a moment, then walked around the gelding to inspect each hoof in turn.

Kate suppressed laughter. She should have known such a meticulous farrier would first want to see if the horse was properly shod.

Finished with his inspection, Bent grunted satisfaction, then, in one lithe movement, swung into the saddle. Flash waited, already saddled on his black-and-white paint quarter horse.

With the help of another cowboy, Kate got the first steer into the chute and, when Bent nodded from the starting box, released the steer.

It ran straight ahead, Bent and Flash thundering on either side. Bent's rope whirled overhead, then snaked out for a clean head catch. In short seconds, Flash had captured the steer's two hind feet with his own rope. The horses whirled to face the steer and each other, signaling the end of the exercise, and Kate cheered. Flash let out a wild whoop and even Bent grinned.

"I told you," Kate yelled happily, dancing a little jig in the dirt. "I told you so!"

Sheer joy and triumph sounded in Flash's laugh. "Don't you hate it when women are right? They always rub it in."

"Damn know-it-all females," Bent growled, his harsh words belied by his grin. "Can't live with 'em, can't kill 'em."

Again Flash laughed while allowing the steer to step out of the loop. Bent released it, as well, and it trotted toward the gate. "Yeah, but I heard about you kissing Kate last night—"

Bent glanced at him sharply as he coiled his rope. "Quick, somebody call the national newspapers. Don't the people of the world have a right to know what the whole damn rodeo crowd already does?" He shook his head in disgust.

"I can see the headlines now," Flash offered. "Former World Champion Rodeo Rider Lovesick Over Up-And-Coming Barrel Racer—"

"Shut up," Kate told them, a high flush staining her cheekbones. Men! They were all idiots. "Both of you, just shut up. If you've got enough energy to gossip like fishwives, then you're not working hard enough. Now put your horses back in the box and get ready for another run."

Both men appeared suitably chagrined. Bent even tipped his hat at her meekly, murmuring, "Yes, ma'am." She wouldn't have been fooled, though, even if she hadn't seen his secretive wink at Flash.

Their first try turned out to be the best run of the night, but later both Bent and Flash were encouraged by their initial success. Sometime after midnight they quit, and Kate was brimming with enthusiasm for the team.

"So?" she asked Bent, smiling broadly as he dismounted.

He lifted one large shoulder. "Flash is doing great. He really is good at heeling. I'm rusty, but...maybe with lots of time, I might become an okay roper. That was fun. But the truth is, I don't have the time or the inclination to devote myself to it."

"You're better than 'okay,'" Kate teased, as usual not giving up. "You're fabulous. You always were and you always will be."

When he turned to her, the now-familiar flame of desire ignited in his eyes. "You think I'm fabulous?"

"Uh-huh." Kate swallowed convulsively, unable to break the almost tangible contact of their connected gaze. With an awkward movement of her hand, she patted the buckskin's sweaty neck. Yet a frisson of warning slid down her spine. Bent obviously knew she was attracted to him. But he could have no idea how deeply that attraction ran. If he ever found out, she realized in a sudden flare of intuition, there would be no keeping him away.

She *must* hold their relationship to a student/teacher basis.

Growing panic made her search frantically for a distracting topic of conversation. "Tell us the story of your triumph at National Finals."

"Would you, Bent?" Flash urged. "I've always wanted to hear the details from you."

Kate could see that, despite himself, Bent was fighting a grin. "Ain't much to tell," he drawled. But she and Flash begged until he relented.

As the two men unsaddled the horses, Bent explained about "going hard" on the circuit that year. About how he had shared single hotel rooms with six other riders to save money, sleeping sometimes on the floor, sometimes in a bathtub. Of how he had flown, driven, and even ridden to more than a hundred rodeos in a great effort to rack up enough points to become one of the deserving few who earned the right to perform at National Finals.

It was a happy day when he rode the bulls and broncs so well at Finals that he earned the glory of becoming All-Around World Champion Cowboy.

"You *are* a true champion," Kate said. She knew her eyes were probably shining her admiration. She knew she probably appeared impossibly young and naive to him at that moment, but she didn't care.

"Nah." Bent grinned at her as he led the horse inside and closed the stall door. "I told you—ole Barry Engan broke his leg in the last performance."

"Engan was a rider?" Flash asked from the next stall, surprised.

"One of the best. I just got lucky." Bent's expression grew thoughtful. "Till his accident, our scores were even. I never did find out if I *could* beat him."

Flash collected a leftover bit of hay from the buckskin's trough and chewed. Slyly, he let a bit of information drop. "Engan's starting to team rope now."

Kate was gratified when Bent's gaze sharpened.

"Yep," Flash continued, seemingly oblivious of Bent's keen interest. "Engan gave up the roughstock riding a few years ago. But he loves 'going down the road,' so he started practicing his calf roping. Grew up on a ranch, like you. Now he's gotten pretty good at team ropin', too. Sometimes gives the top men a run for their money."

Wisely, Flash said no more, and Kate was grateful for the sensitive youth. If she'd tried to casually drop such information, Bent would definitely be suspicious. But Flash could get away with it. She smiled to herself, well satisfied. The seed had been planted.

The circuit was a difficult grind, but Kate endured the bad food, little sleep and hours of driving as best she could. She used maps and got directions from seasoned riders to the cow towns and backwaters and whistle-stops as well as to the big cities. For the first time in her life, she got a taste of America's heartland.

Aboard Sierra, all the travel and effort faded away and she knew the joy of the wind's cool fingers gliding through her hair. Looking forward to seeing Bent at three-week intervals helped. His coaching improved her times considerably, and as summer drew on she got to know Sarah, as well.

Once a week she called home to Mimi, giving the results of her competitions and discussing her standings. She must finish the year in the top fifteen to go to National Finals. As yet, she hadn't quite made it, but there were months left, with several important competitions coming up, and she was already close.

At night when she bedded down, Kate had moments of doubt. Was she crazy to take Mimi's long-saved money and gamble on a near-impossible goal? Maybe her father had been right about her. After all, he'd been a champion steer wrestler himself. He'd known rodeo; he'd known what it took.

Why hadn't he seen a champion when he'd looked at his own daughter? What was she missing?

You don't have what it takes. He'd thrown the words at her with casual cruelty. He'd known how badly she'd wanted to race. *Why, Daddy?* Kate whispered one dark night. *Why?*

Kate closed her eyes and prayed.

In the daily grind, caring for Sierra took a great deal of time—from feeding her special vitamins and minerals, to wrapping her legs, to checking her hooves and making sure she wasn't overworked or going sour.

Over the Fourth of July Cowboy Christmas, so called because of the many competitions put on during the holiday week, she rushed to six different rodeos. From Greeley, Colorado, she traveled to Eugene, Oregon, and included many other stops in between. At the end of the week Kate was both pleased with her successes and exhausted at the same time.

Deciding to take a much-needed five days off and go home to Riverside, Kate telephoned Bent to let him know. "How's Sierra?" he asked before asking how Kate herself was.

"Tired," Kate answered, trying not to wince at his concern for the horse taking precedence over his concern for her. After all, that was his job. She should not take it personally. "She needs to just doze in a sunny pasture, roll in the dirt. Rest."

"Sounds like you need that, too," he guessed.

"Yeah, rolling in the dirt sounds terrific."

"I meant the part about the rest, grumpy."

"Ah, so you do care," she needled him.

"Sure. Gotta keep my meal ticket going strong."

Kate strangled back several unladylike names she'd like to yell at him. She was calling on a roadside pay phone at the last rodeo town and it looked like rain. With a weary hand she adjusted the receiver closer to her ear.

"Just kidding," Bent said at her prolonged silence. "Where are you?"

Glancing out the glass windows of the phone booth, Kate felt a moment's confusion. There was a grocery store, a hardware store, cars passing on the street. Suddenly the place looked like so many others she'd been in lately. "I don't know. I...forgot."

"Man, you are ready for a rest. Maybe I'll come down to Riverside and take you out for a nice dinner."

"Dinner?" She felt her brows arch.

"Yeah. That's the meal you eat when it gets dark."

"Don't get sarcastic, cowboy. It's just, well, you threw me. It sounds like a date."

"So it is." His voice was low, husky-edged, but warm. Somehow it was exactly what Kate needed right then. Maybe he *did* care about her.

Yet something puzzled her. "But—I thought, well—"

"You thought what?"

She frowned, wondering how to phrase her question. Too tired to think of a tactful way, she bit her lip and merely blurted it out. "It seems like you just want to haul me into bed—forget the dinner and conversation."

"If you'd like it that way," he said dryly, "it can be arranged."

"Bent!"

"Take it easy, Katie girl. All I want is dinner. You can even sit on the opposite side of the table from me, okay?"

She sighed, wanting more than anything to see him. Without him, she'd been lonely. "Just dinner?"

"For now."

She couldn't help but give a soft laugh. "Fair enough."

"It'll have to be before the weekend, though. Sarah's thirteenth birthday is on Saturday."

"It is? Why don't we have a party for her instead?"

"A party?" he said uncertainly. "I don't know—"

"Sure, it'll be great," she went on, warming to her subject. It would do Sarah good to have some special attention. "You can bring your mom and Sarah. I'll invite Flash and some of the new friends Sarah's made from the circuit."

"Mimi won't mind having her house turned into a zoo?"

"She'll love it. It's all settled. We'll do an outdoor barbecue. You're in charge of cooking the meat. We'll do the rest."

There was a pause on the telephone. For a second Kate thought the line had gone dead. Then Bent said simply, "Thanks, Kate. This'll mean a lot to Sarah. You really have been good for her. And good *to* her."

The grateful sincerity in his voice went straight to her heart. When he chose, the man could be devastating.

With the party set for three o'clock on Saturday, Kate spent the morning rushing around Riverside picking up orange, blue and pink helium balloons and party napkins and plates of matching colors. Mimi went off to the supermarket for food, immediately enthusiastic about the party. She planned to serve potato chips, ambrosia fruit salad, hot dogs and hamburgers as well as a luscious chocolate layer cake she'd baked herself.

When Bent, his mother Tess and Sarah drove up at noon, Kate was waiting impatiently. She'd dressed in new blue jeans, a crimson-yoked shirt and wide leather belt, which cinched tight at her waist and showed off her narrow hips and flat belly. Hurriedly, she tucked a loose strand of hair back into her braid.

Bent got out of his truck, grumbling, "I don't see why we had to get here so early. I could've done some work around the house."

Kate heard him, but his words barely registered. Despite his complaints, his eyes captured and held hers. It seemed like months since she'd seen him, years, and to her starved vision, he was a treat.

Wear-faded jeans clung to his powerful legs. A long-sleeved, Western shirt of muted deep amber fitted well over his broad shoulders and matched his impossibly hued eyes. There was even a bolo tie at his neck. On his head his silver-gray hat was firmly clamped. Tanned, the picture of health, he could be a Western model stepping out of a cigarette ad.

Something deep inside Kate went intensely focused—acutely aware—like during those few seconds after the rodeo announcer called her name and just before she gave Sierra the signal to go.

Words of greeting escaped Kate and she discovered her mouth had gone dry. "You—you need a belt and buckle to finish your outfit," she said inanely.

He shrugged. "I don't wear the buckles anymore."

"Maybe you will—someday—for me?"

Eyes narrowing, his gaze lasered through her like probing sensual fingers that sought out all her hidden, sensitive places.

Sarah had already tumbled out, squealing when she saw the bouquets of helium balloons, and ran up the front porch steps to squeal again when she saw a small pile of prettily wrapped birthday gifts. She wore a new pair of denims and one of the more feminine tops Kate had helped her choose. Bent turned to help his mother out of the truck.

Tall, graying Tess immediately reminded Kate of Mimi, though the two did not look alike. Tess came forward and took one of Kate's hands in both her own.

"Kate. It's sweet of you to have this party for Sarah, and she's so excited. I'm glad to meet you."

"Welcome." Kate smiled, liking the woman's warm greeting. Tess's hair was kept in a short, no-nonsense bob, and she wore teal slacks, an overblouse and no makeup. Humor lines radiated from the edges of her eyes. "Mimi is looking forward to meeting you. She's baking in the kitchen right now."

"Say no more. I'm off to help her." Leaning back inside the truck, she collected a bag of chips, salsa and a big loaf of French bread, then hurried into the house.

Bent faced Kate sardonically. "Well, I'm here. Now what are you going to do with me until the party starts?"

"Do with you? How about a beer?"

He shook his head. "Too early. How about a kiss?"

"Too early." She edged away. "How about a soda?"

He laughed.

"Flash'll be over soon," she assured him, "and you two can make use of that old roping dummy that's in the pasture where I work Sierra. Or you could outdo each other's roping tricks."

"You're bound and determined to keep me roping, aren't you, Kate? Why?"

"Why not?" Maybe bravado would work.

He blinked and she smiled at him. "I don't care what you do today, Benton Murray. You're a grown man, you'll think of something to amuse yourself. But Sarah and I are leaving—we have appointments. That's why you had to come early."

"What kind of appointments?"

"You'll see."

"Uh-huh. Sounds like it's going to cost me money." Resigned, he withdrew his wallet and opened it.

"How'd you guess?" Smiling, Kate held out her hand. "I figure it'll be about a hundred dollars. You know, I think I like it better this way—you paying me instead of me paying you. Except this money is for Sarah, isn't it? Someday perhaps I could teach you something. Then you could pay *me.*"

"What could you teach me?" He crossed his arms, his feet spread arrogantly wide.

How to love. The thought sprang into her mind unbidden and completely unexpected. For several seconds, it rocked her. The idea was crazy, unwanted. Frightening.

Chapter Six

Sarah appeared on the porch steps, shading her eyes against the noon sun. "Ready, Kate?"

"Let's go." Grateful for the interruption, she brushed a hand over her eyes as if to brush away the disturbing notion, and headed for her pickup.

Bent frowned at the two females. "Is this gonna take long?"

Kate opened the truck door and slid one jeans-clad leg inside while Sarah got into the passenger side. Suppressing a smile, she pretended to think. "Let's put it this way. If we're not back in, say, three hours...?"

"Yeah?"

"Then just wait longer." She drove away with Sarah giggling in her ear.

At the beauty parlor Kate, Sarah and the hairstylist conferred on the best trim for Sarah's thick hair. Clouds of hairspray, the heat of hair dryers, and the noise of a dozen chatting women filled the room.

"You have such pretty brown eyes—like warm chocolate," the stylist remarked thoughtfully to Sarah. "Let's feather your bangs and get the hair off your face so the boys can see those peepers, hmm?"

Sarah flushed and cast an inquiring glance at Kate, to which she gave an encouraging nod.

"Okay." Sarah squirmed in the chair looking self-conscious, and Kate gave her another reassuring smile. The poor girl had apparently never been pampered in this way before. Sarah was much loved by Tess and Bent, Kate had no doubt of that. But somehow Sarah's rites of maturity had escaped her grandmother and father.

"I think," Kate suggested, "a jaw-length cut. Perhaps right to here." She indicated a spot at the base of Sarah's smooth neck.

"Do you?" Sarah fingered the ragged ends of her shoulder-length hair. "It's always been long."

"It's a good idea, honey," the stylist said. "It'll be smart-looking and fit right in with what the teenagers are doing now."

"And easy to maintain," Kate added.

Sarah agreed, and after submitting to shampooing, cutting and blow-drying, she was thrilled. She kept staring in the mirror at her new shining coiffure as it swung saucily against her cheeks. Afterward, Kate led her to the manicurist's table and watched indulgently while the lady carefully buffed and painted Sarah's finger and toenails.

At last a makeup artist instructed a fascinated Sarah on makeup for a young girl. "A subtle application of mascara, a bit of peach blush and lip gloss," the young operator explained, "is best. There's nothing worse than seeing globs of black eyeliner ringing a thirteen-year-old girl's eyes—or bloodred lipstick and reddish rouge." She gave a delicate shiver. "Like Frankenstein's bride. Yech!"

Kate and Sarah laughed and Sarah quietly allowed the procedure. She shyly agreed to let Kate use Bent's money to buy some of the lip gloss and mascara.

They left the establishment with Sarah beaming and Kate pleased with the outcome of her afternoon plans.

"We have one more stop to make," Kate announced, leading Sarah toward a tiny jeweler's shop. An ornate wrought iron window framed rows of watches, rings and bracelets under sparkling lights. "If you like, we can have your ears pierced today."

Wide-eyed, the girl peered into the window. "I'd love it," she exclaimed, then hesitated. "But Daddy—"

"I got his permission by telephone last week—it's okay," Kate assured her. "He said—" she drew herself up importantly, assumed a dour expression, and lowered her voice like a man's "—as long as you don't bring my daughter home tattooed, I don't mind."

Sarah giggled. "That'd be funny. Let's go get one of those temporary tattoos and fool him."

Kate winced, picturing his reaction. "Somehow I don't think he'd get the joke. We'd better stick with ear piercing."

"Okay," she said, giving up the tattoo with reluctance. "But what about earrings? I don't have any."

"The jeweler will give you gold posts till your ears heal. Then...well, maybe you'd best see what's in some of those birthday packages sitting on the porch."

Curiously, Sarah didn't react, and Kate wondered if something was wrong. Had she taken too much for granted, arranging all these appointments and gussying the girl up? Long seconds passed and Kate was about to ask what was amiss when Sarah abruptly threw herself into Kate's arms and clung to her neck.

"Thank you, Kate. You're cool." Her eyes misty, Sarah squeezed Kate for a moment, then flung open the jeweler's door and bounced inside.

Hesitating a moment, Kate smiled slowly. Such gratitude in a youth of Sarah's age was rare indeed. Bent and Tess truly had done a wonderful job with her, and she was pleased and honored to be trusted so willingly by her. She found herself blinking several times before she followed the girl inside.

Everyone was in good spirits when they returned, with Tess and Mimi in a friendly boasting competition about their grandchildren. When Kate arrived, letting the made-over Sarah enter the house first, a hush fell between the two elderly women.

Tess came forward, laying a palm along the girl's cheek. "Wow! What a terrific change!"

"Yes, you look fabulous," Mimi heartily agreed. "Just right for your birthday party. Would you like to frost your own cake? I've got strawberry or chocolate icing."

"Chocolate, I guess." Sarah smiled anxiously. "Do you really like how I look? You don't think it's too... different, do you?"

Bent wandered into the kitchen after a soda. Seeing Sarah, he pulled up short.

Kate waited, knowing Sarah was holding her breath for her father's reaction, knew how badly the girl wanted his approval.

A low wolf whistle, a grin, and a quick hug eased Sarah's fears—and Kate's. "Sarah, you're growing up on me, aren't you, sweetheart?" he asked.

"Yes, Daddy," she said in a small voice.

Everyone smiled.

"Goodness, you do look different," Mimi boomed, breaking the spell. "Kate's helped you bring out your natural beauty. That's what being a woman's all about. Making the most of your potential—and looks are a part of that. Why, I remember the first time I took Kate to a beauty parlor, she—"

"Not now, Mimi," Kate warned, hands on hips.

"Kate! You're not *still* embarrassed about how the beginning stylist colored your hair pink when you merely wanted a touch of blond?"

Much to Sarah and Tess's amusement, Kate rolled her eyes. "All right, all right. Since you insist on letting the entire state know about it, my head looked like a poof of cotton candy for weeks, okay? I looked awful. There. I've said it." In mock consternation, she crossed her arms and tapped a booted toe. "Anything *else* you want to tell?"

Mimi rounded her eyes innocently. "Oh, you mean like when—"

"Stop," Kate demanded. "Sarah, I think it's time you frosted that cake before all my skeletons are rattled out of the closet. Excuse me." Behind her came sounds of smothered snickering. She felt very good-natured in ignoring them.

In the backyard Kate and Bent found Flash, as well as two young barrel racers Sarah had befriended and a rodeo clown friend of Bent's. In the afternoon breeze the balloons blew gently while Flash demonstrated his roping tricks. Bent took a seat atop the split-rail fence.

"I'm not as good as Bent," Flash told the small crowd humbly when they applauded, and he tried to hand the rope over to the farrier.

From his position on the fence, Bent staved him off with an upraised hand. "No, thank you."

"Aw, come on," Flash urged.

"Not in the mood. Sorry." Bent shrugged, grinning. He had refused, Kate was sure, so he wouldn't upstage Flash. Warmth crept through her veins like thick honey. This was the Benton Murray she was drawn to. This was the man she found so hard to resist.

To Flash, he offered encouragement. "You're not a great roper, Flash—yet. But you could be. You've got the drive." His voice quieted and he turned briefly introspective. "I admire that."

"You do?" Flash looked puzzled. "But you're a world champion. I haven't won anything."

Bent smiled. "You're young yet." He jumped down from the fence. "While I'm here, I want to check on Sierra's bar shoe, see if it's still helping that quarter crack. Want to come?"

"Sure." Flash coiled his rope and followed. The entire party ended up at the small barn and watched while Bent explained the intricacies of applying a pad and bar shoe to alleviate the pressure of the healing hoof crack. Flash was suddenly fascinated. Before five minutes had passed, Kate noticed he had asked innumerable questions about shoeing, and she appreciated it when Bent answered each one.

"Horseshoeing is interpretive, not an exact science," Bent explained patiently. "Ideally, there should be open communication between the owner, the vet and the farrier, with input about the horse from all three.''

Flash grinned. ''Like a three-way marriage?''

Bent burst out laughing and clapped the youth on the back. ''Sure. Kind of like that.'' Leaning an arm against Sierra's flank, he said, ''A good farrier is a perfectionist, but there's never a perfect job—we aren't Mother Nature. Now, watch while I trim this hoof for proper balance.'' He gestured Flash closer and the young man moved forward willingly.

In the end Mimi and Tess had to threaten, then almost drag Flash to the picnic area to help set up tables. Later Bent barbecued the hamburgers and hot dogs outside. As the afternoon waned, they ate, everyone exclaiming over the delicious food, Sarah the happiest of all.

When the party had eaten full to bursting, the rodeo clown sat down to share entertaining stories of wild bulls and near-death escapes from gouging horns and slashing hooves. Bent let the coals die in the barbecue and turned to Kate, spatula in hand. ''Sarah's happy,'' he remarked simply. ''And she looks so pretty. Guess I owe you thanks again.''

''Seeing her so thrilled is all the thanks I need.'' Kate surveyed the mess of food, napkins and plates that littered the tables and knew she ought to begin cleaning up. But she was reluctant to leave Bent's side. He was more relaxed than she'd ever seen him, his smile quick.

''Want to take a walk?'' he suggested, as if he could read her mind.

''Sure.'' She gestured toward Sierra's barn. ''Come into my office.''

He chuckled, putting down the spatula and letting his hand rest at the small of her back. They walked together through tall weeds, past low-hanging trees. Fading sunshine was soft on her shoulders. For once the ever-present sexual tension between them was banked. The bay mare lifted her head inquiringly over the side of her stall, whinnying softly to Kate. "Not today, Sierra," Kate called to her. "The boss says you need rest."

"That's right," Bent agreed with her, arrogant tyrant that he was, "and you always obey the boss."

"Yes, boss," Kate replied meekly, feeling a mischievous smile tug at the corners of her mouth. "Anything you say, boss. We aim to please, boss—"

"Enough," he ordered gruffly, and Kate couldn't resist a last "Yes, boss."

He slanted a grin down at her and squeezed her waist warmly. She stopped at the first barrel of her practice course and tapped the rusting top with her short fingernails. "I love to barrel race," she mused, studying the triangular-shaped groove worn into the ground around the three oil drums. "I love it so much I can't understand why everyone in the world doesn't want to experience the glorious feel of the wind in their face."

Bent kicked a rock out of the groove. "To each his own."

"Did you ever try it yourself?" she wondered, rounding the barrel so it stood between them.

"Sure I did. Had to know what it felt like to train Maria Vendala and those others."

A thought came to her. "Did you ever have, uh, a romantic relationship with Maria?"

"Nah." He picked a long blade of grass and chewed it between his teeth. "I was married," he said, as if that explained it all.

"Maria was very beautiful."

"You're beautiful."

She blushed lightly, refusing to be sidetracked. "I've noticed a lot of rodeo riders don't seem to care much about honoring their marriage vows."

"I did."

She nodded, believing him. "That's good." Somehow knowing that when Bent made a vow he would keep it pleased her immeasurably. She didn't know why it should do so, because they would never really become romantically involved. "Someday," she went on in the same musing tone, "I hope to become as great a rider as Maria."

"You've the talent, Kate."

"Do you think so?" She never tired of hearing his praise.

"Know so." The creases beside his eyes crinkled with laughter.

For some reason she thought of Sarah. "You know Sarah wants to race, don't you?"

The air between them changed; she could feel it when he stiffened, could feel his swift loss of humor. "So?"

"So, why don't you let her?"

Later, she would come to regret her baldly stated question.

"No," he growled low and harsh. "And don't ask again. It's none of your business."

Kate hated the clipped rudeness in his tone, hated the hurt that sliced through her at the abrupt way he so casually cut her out of his life. Dropping her chin to her chest, she pretended to study her thumbnail.

An awkward silence vibrated the sunlit air between them while a metallic-green dragonfly zoomed past on his business. She'd be damned if she would be the one to break the quiet.

After long moments she heard Bent draw a deep breath as he reached over the barrel to touch her arm. "I'm not used to explaining. I guess I shouldn't bite your head off." She watched while he squinted into some middle distance, struggling for words. She remained silent, letting him take his time.

"Remember I told you I don't want to be involved in rodeo? Well, I don't want my daughter involved, either. My wife..." he said with obvious difficulty. "I quit—"

"After she left you?" Kate guessed shrewdly. "But why?"

Half turning away, Bent tilted his head just enough so that his hat shielded his face from her. "I don't have good memories of rodeo."

She was aghast. "Don't have good memories? How can that be? You won so much—you were so talented—so magnetic! I *saw* you win at National Finals. I *saw* what a competitor you were."

A lowering frown drew his brows together. "Look—forget it—"

"Don't you see?" she rushed on, suddenly feeling as if she could now understand much of what made Bent the reserved man he'd become. The dragonfly made another pass and she waved it away with an impatient hand. "You're blaming a *sport,* for heaven's sake, for the failure of your marriage."

"Damn it, Kate. I'm not gonna talk about—"

"You can rope, and you love it—don't deny that." Filled with enthusiastic zeal, she ignored the dangerous narrowing of his eyes. "Bent, I could see it on your face. Besides, you *are* involved in rodeo. With me. Sarah wants to compete. Are you going to stop her forever?"

"If that's what it takes," he vowed.

"Sarah isn't a baby anymore, but a young lady whose world is broadening. You saw it today. She needs something in her life she can aspire to. A subject or sport in school."

Bent listened, an angry, unhappy twist to his mouth. She could see him thinking, but he would concede nothing. "I'm gonna be a rancher, Kate. In Montana. I don't need rodeo."

She heard only one word. "*Montana?*"

"Yeah. I told you I'm saving for a ranch. I want to raise quarter horses, Angus cattle."

"But... I thought... that is, I assumed you meant California." In Montana he would be so far away she'd never see him. The idea was shocking and unpleasant. All at once she felt her enthusiasm to fight for Sarah's rights drain away like water out of a punctured horse trough.

Needing time to digest this bombshell, she walked a few steps away. When she turned back, she noticed the sun was setting behind him, making it difficult to read his expression until a shift in balance brought his features into focus.

He was staring at her with more than his usual intensity, his desire for her crowding out all other considerations, and she felt an answering fire ignite within herself.

"Would you care, Kate?" he asked softly. "If I moved away?"

"Well, of course," she murmured, struggling for an explanation. "I'd miss Sarah terribly. And I've become, uh, fond of you, despite your bad temperament."

"Nice," he said, even more gently, advancing on her around the barrel. "I'm flattered."

Kate didn't realize she'd been retreating until her back bumped into the split-rail fence. Once again, she felt trapped by Bent's unwavering gaze and big, powerful body. Deliciously so.

She held her hand out, palm flat on his chest. "No, Bent," she tried to protest, but found laying a hand on him was a mistake. The strong thunder of his heartbeat pulsed against her fingertips. Try as she might to ignore it, she enjoyed the warmth of his skin through his shirt. She felt as if his very lifeblood was calling to her, his heartbeat seeking to match the escalating rhythm of her own.

Something in her manner must have given her away, some telltale flicker of her eyes. Or perhaps it was a minute shift in her body temperature he was sensitive to, because with a movement as natural as breathing, he raised a hand to her shoulder, then caught the end of her braid to run between his hard fingers. In an almost offhand tone, he said, "I'm not sure I can keep my hands off you, Kate." Causing her further discomfort, he managed to read her thoughts. "And I don't think you want me to, either."

She stared back, desperate to avoid his mesmerizing eyes by resting her gaze safely on his strong jaw. Yet it wasn't so safe when in seconds she was wondering at the texture of his skin, wondering how it would feel against her cheek or nuzzled at the delicate junction of her neck and shoulder.

How might it feel if they lay together in a twisted tangle of sheets, and he were to run his face down her spine?

At the erotic image, she felt goose bumps rise and tried to suppress a shiver.

Breathing deeply in an effort to calm herself, she took in his scent of horse and leather and unique skin fragrance. It heightened her awareness of him even more.

She'd tried so hard to hide her feelings, but he was as attuned to her as she was to him. When he took her into his arms, she melted, responded with a depth of emotion that overwhelmed her. The man was larger than life—a champion.

Her champion.

Bent's kiss was everything and more than she remembered, full of energy and hungry passion, like the wildest, most headlong ride imaginable. His hard-callused hands held her head and he kissed her with exquisite care, nibbling along her lower lip while her eyes drifted shut. He touched the bow of her upper lip with his tongue, then, gaining entrance into her mouth, deepened the caress until blood coursed through her veins and her heart pounded like thundering hooves.

Alarmingly, her knees started to wobble.

As if from far away, a soft trill of laughter came from the house and Kate's eyes snapped open. Sarah and her friends were coming, probably looking for them.

"I don't guess this is the best place for this," Bent noted wryly, still holding her. He gestured around the open field with reluctant humor. Then his smile faded. "Anyway, it's not a good idea."

Kate blinked, wriggling to get free of his arms, desperate to collect her muddled senses. She wondered if he had any idea how insulting it was for him to practically apologize for kissing her. A slow anger started to simmer, replacing the weak wanting. "Oh, it's my *youth* again, is it? Maybe I should go play with a pail and shovel."

At last disentangling herself from him, she glared into his frowning face and knew she'd hit the shoeing nail on the head. Eyes burning into him, she challenged him silently to refute his hang-up on the issue of their age difference. His frown merely deepened, his lack of response conspicuous.

There seemed nothing left to say, so she simply pushed past him and headed toward the house.

Walking away from him was one of the most difficult things she'd ever done. Her steps were stiff, jerky, her facial muscles frozen. She didn't want Bent guilt-ridden over kissing her because of her "youth." She didn't want to deal with his swift mood changes and frequent bouts of off-putting bitterness over something for which she was not responsible.

But she wanted his kiss. Lord help her, she did want that.

Back with the others, she forced a smile and, with Tess and Mimi's help, began cleaning up the paper plates and food. She smiled more and nodded as Sarah opened her gifts. Hopefully her face wouldn't crack off.

It was obvious Sarah's favorite gifts were the two pair of earrings Kate had bought her—small gold hoops and tiny pearl posts. It gratified Kate to see the happiness shining from the girl's eyes. And it took some of the sting from Bent's comments.

Through it all, Bent said nothing to her, but she could feel the heat of his dissatisfied gaze; it seemed never to leave her. She did her best to ignore him. They ate cake and ice cream and eventually everyone began to leave.

It was full dark when Bent bade good-night to Mimi and the exhausted woman went into the house. Last thank-yous were called to Kate from Tess and Sarah as they got into the truck. Bent lingered outside, fussing an unnecessarily long time arranging Sarah's packages in the pickup's bed. Kate watched from the steps of the porch.

Twisting her hands together, she didn't know if she desperately wanted him to leave or recklessly wanted him to stay. Confusion and mixed emotions swirled in her head, made her grit her teeth with a kind of waiting tension.

She didn't know what she was waiting for until she saw Bent assure himself his mother and daughter were ensconced in the truck and then stride deliberately toward her. Her heart rate accelerated. Was he going to kiss her good night? And in front of Tess and Sarah? They could see from the closed windows of the truck, but they couldn't hear.

When he came to a halt on the ground two steps below her, he tipped back his hat. "We're not going home. Tess is tired and it's too far to drive tonight. I'm taking them to a local motel. But I'll be back here. At midnight."

Kate gasped.

He turned to go, and she watched, stunned. "By the way," he finished, "you won't need your pail and shovel."

With that he slammed into his vehicle, backed up and sped off into the night, gravel flying.

Mimi retired by ten-thirty, while a keyed-up Kate cleaned a bit more, eyes cling to the clock. Bent *couldn't* really mean to return and resume their lover's embrace? Each time she thought about the possibilities, her face grew hot and her hands so clumsy she dropped two glasses and fumbled with the leftover cake.

Her gaze swung again to the clock. It was exactly one minute later. Would he come? She peered out the front window into the darkness. Nothing.

In her bedroom she gave in to impulse and changed into a fresh shirt. At the hall mirror, she fussed with the collar of the forest green flannel shirt and tucked a loose strand of hair into her braid. She checked her teeth to see if there were any spinach leaves stuck, even though there had been no spinach served, and was halfway through brushing her teeth when sharp impatience took hold.

What was she doing, primping for Benton Murray? He couldn't just highhandedly haul her out of her house and kiss the boots off her anytime he wished!

Her outrage lasted right up until she heard the low rumble of his truck pull up out front. At that moment her anger, along with her courage, abruptly fled.

She opened the door a crack, then, spying his truck, crept quietly onto the porch. In the glow of a lone yard lamp, he stood pooled—a figure spotlighted in the darkness. He waited, leaning against his hood, legs and arms negligently crossed, hat pulled characteristically low.

Kate found her voice. "Go away," she whispered.

"Come with me," he commanded in return.

"No."

"Get down here or I'll come after you."

Helpless, she shook her head.

With no hesitation, he straightened and strode toward her. When his hard-soled boot hit the lowest step with a bang, she hastened toward him, afraid Mimi would wake with the sound. "Damn it, Bent, you can't—"

He grasped her wrist, his hold like a handcuff, and towed her around the house toward her practice area where they'd kissed earlier. It was even darker away from the yard lights, the trees creepily reaching out fingers to snatch at their clothes. Weeds damp from evening condensation brushed against their boots. Crickets called for mates and an owl hooted a warning to the night creatures. In the dark Kate felt nearly blind, but Bent appeared to know exactly where he was going. He became her beacon, her touchstone in the inkiness. She stumbled and was forced to cling to him, instead of pushing him away.

"Wait, Bent. We can't," she managed to say.

"Shh."

This time he brushed past the barrels, went through a gate and didn't stop until they were sheltered from view beneath the branches of a low-hanging oak.

Teeth dug into her lip, Kate felt herself trembling, though the night was warm. Against her will, she realized it was thrilling to be stolen away by a strong, romantic man. "What—" she began, her breath so short she ran out of air and had to start again. "What are you going to do?"

"This," he said simply, gathering her swiftly into his arms and kissing her. His passion tonight was almost violent, and despite her reservations, Kate knew a matching need. It took only an instant before thought faded away, replaced by emotion. Low in her throat, she moaned. She thrust her hands into his hair, toppling his hat, helplessly showing him all her pent-up desire.

It was too late for rational thinking, she realized as he built the sexual net of desire around her. Much too late.

Chapter Seven

Beneath the arms of the sheltering old oak, Bent struggled to hold Kate gently and not crush her to him in a fury of need and desire. She was so soft, so accommodating, so feminine. Holding Kate made him want to take up roughstock riding again—to get on a rank bull and ride him to a quivering standstill. She made him feel powerful and full of life.

For months now he'd tried and tried to keep his hands off her. She wasn't for him, he knew that. Someday she'd find a young man her own age, someone who suited her, not someone broken down and jaded like him. He should never have touched her.

Too late.

Once he'd put his hands on her this evening—and now tonight—he was caught in a great, unstoppable landslide. Nothing he could do would prevent the crashing together of their bodies.

He hardly realized he was muttering her name over and over until she answered in a vague, passion-drenched voice. *She wanted him as badly as he wanted her.* The realization swept through his system like wildfire.

He couldn't take his mouth off her body. At the delicate skin of her neck, he nuzzled her. On her chin, he planted kisses before moving along the line of her jaw, then on to nibble her earlobe.

When, in the natural course of things, his mouth lowered to her collarbone and continued down to burrow into the valley between her breasts, he was surprised when she gasped.

"I—I can't do this," she cried, passion warring with anguish in her tone. "Don't you see? I . . . can't."

"Shh," he murmured, a great urge to protect and comfort her welling within him. "Don't worry, honey. I know I haven't earned the right yet. After Finals . . ."

She pushed on his chest, forcing an inch between them. It felt like a mile. "'After Finals'?" she wondered aloud, still bemused, and he chuckled, enjoying her muddled confusion. *He'd* created this reaction in her, and it made him feel pleased and proud.

"I haven't earned the right yet to be your lover," he assured her with a squeeze. "Don't worry. I know that."

She blinked, beginning to struggle in his arms which, instead of loosening, clamped around her. "You think . . . that by coaching me . . . I can be bought?" Outrage framed her words and quickly he sought ways to soothe her.

"It's all right. You can trust me. I won't do anything you don't want." Reaching up, he massaged her shoulders. "Whatever happens between us will be shared—not forced. Do you understand? Your pleasure will be mine."

She stared into his eyes, some of the suspicion fading away. "You're sure about that? You won't push me?"

"Of course not. I'm not an animal."

"No," she agreed slowly. "You're not."

"Trust me. Let me touch you. I won't go too far, I swear it." Without waiting for a reply, he deftly drew his fingers along the buttoned opening of her shirt. Smiling into her eyes, he stroked the upper slope of her breast. "You're so pretty, Kate. I wish I could see you."

"See me? You—you mean—nude?" She shivered and he couldn't help chuckling again.

"Mmm" was his reply. "I'll bet you look delicious."

Her laughter was reluctant but honest. Her head bent forward shyly. "No. My legs are too skinny and I'm not very, uh, endowed—"

"Endowed? Honey, everything looks just fine to me." Deliberately he lowered his gaze to her firm breasts, letting her see by his expression how much he appreciated them.

She flushed. "Well, anyway, I have two moles on my..." Her voice trailed off and she blinked again, as if surprised at revealing so much.

"Where are your moles?"

Her lips firmed and at his chest her palms flattened. "Never mind. I can't believe I almost told you that."

Deep in his chest, new laughter rumbled. "I'll find out."

"Not tonight, you won't."

"No," he hastened to agree. "Not tonight." Running his fingers lightly down her arms and back up again, he asked, "You like my hands on your body, don't you, Kate?"

"I..."

He refused to help her, only lifted a brow.

"All right," she capitulated suddenly. "I do. But that doesn't mean—"

"Is it okay if I touch you here?" Again he ran his hands from her upper arms down to her wrists. When she nodded, he moved to her neck, fingers splayed at either side of her throat and partway down her chest. Making tiny motions, he caressed her skin through her shirt. "Here?"

Again she nodded. Her eyelids fluttered shut and her breathing escalated. He found he could look at her all night, intensely enjoying the gradual softening of her features as she allowed his touch. The soft light of the moon filtered through the branches, lovingly outlining her delicate features—hints of how she must look in the throes of full passion, he realized, and the sight heated his blood to near boiling.

Yet he gritted his teeth and swore he would go slow. He had no wish to frighten her or break his word. He must deny the impulses hammering at him to claim her body and sear his imprint on her so deeply she never wanted to look at another man. At least for a while.

His smile deepened. That promise did not preclude taking preliminary pleasures, or from giving her a taste of what their eventual, inevitable joining would be like.

Easing open the buttons of her shirt, he slipped his hand inside and cupped her breast, finding her upraised nipple easily through her serviceable white bra.

"You like it when I touch you here." It was a statement, without any question in his mind.

Murmuring something unintelligible against his chest, she sighed, then just as quickly drew in new breath. Behind her back, he slid his hands under her shirt, then unlatched her bra. Her naked breasts spilled into his hands and his own breath caught in wonder.

Rational thought became a thing of the past as he groaned, bending to capture one nipple in his mouth. He teased it with his teeth and tongue, then drew on it so the skin puckered and pebbled for him.

Kate's legs shifted and wobbled, and he realized that her body was urging her to lie down—nature's way of making the female more accessible for lovemaking.

Eager to accommodate her, Bent swept her up high against his chest, and then, taking her mouth in a searing kiss, lowered them both into the soft weeds. With his arm behind her neck, her head fell back. He reached up to remove the elastic that held the end of her braid, then loosened her hair so the strands glowing golden in the moonlight fell in waves over his arm.

Lying beside her, he flung a leg across both of hers and spread his hand possessively across her bare stomach. Her arms wound tightly around his neck, pulling him down for a long, luxurious kiss.

All the while, his hands caressed her, stroked her, and he was careful with the gift of her surrender. Even if it wasn't complete, he was too grateful for this heaven-sent boon to complain. Kate was here—moon-bathed and beautiful and eager for his touch.

Never had he felt such reverence for a woman, such desire. Smart, sassy, never-say-die Kate was finally his to pet and pamper, and he wanted her to feel pleasure more than he wanted his own. When he lightly abraded her nipples again, she moaned. And he smiled.

"Bent," she whispered against his mouth. "Bent, I can't think."

He smiled, drunk with her. "That's the idea."

"Can *you* think?"

"Yes. I'm completely clear on what I want." He proceeded to show her with a graphic demonstration by moving his groin against her thigh. "I'm thinking I'd like to have my hands all over you—not just on a few small parts. I'm thinking of stripping off your jeans and shirt and underwear until you're uncovered and open for me." He lowered his voice to a husky drawl. "I'm thinking I want you solidly beneath me, bucking like a wild mare."

"Oh," she said breathlessly, then bit her lip. "Wow."

He grinned. "Yeah, wow."

Before he could react, she sat up, brushing her hair from her eyes. "Maybe I'd better go in." With shaking fingers, she caught the edges of her blouse and brought them together. She began to shake the weeds from her clothes.

He frowned, hating her withdrawal. "You're not afraid of me, are you?"

"Yes—no. Oh, I don't know." Her brows furrowed as she concentrated. "It's not you, Bent. It's me. I'm afraid of me."

Sitting up beside her, he repositioned his hat. "I don't get it."

"I—I'm scared of what I might do if... if I get carried away."

Mood lightening, Bent smiled. He liked the idea of Kate getting "carried away."

While he was thinking of some interesting possibilities, she surprised him by getting to her feet.

He got up, too. "Don't go."

She adjusted her clothing, then laid her hand on his chest in a manner that was fast becoming a habit. He didn't mind it at all. "Look, if I stay here with you any longer, things will get out of hand—"

He grinned wolfishly. "No, I'll definitely keep 'things' in hand."

"Funny." She scowled at him. "Anyway, I guess it's no secret to you that I think you're handsome as the devil and twice as sexy. You see—" She bit her lip and chanced a quick look into his face, as if uncertain whether to go on.

"What is it, honey?" He couldn't let her stop now.

"When I was twelve years old, younger than Sarah is now, I watched you win National Finals."

Reluctantly he buttoned an opening she'd missed on her shirt. "Yes, sweetheart. I know."

"Well, imagine the changes Sarah's going through now. Pretty soon, if she doesn't already, she's going to start liking boys. I liked them at twelve."

He wasn't sure where she was going, but he wasn't about to stop her. She looked stunning with tree-filtered moonlight dappled on her skin, the light catching her bright hair and making intriguing hollows of her cheeks and collarbone. "Uh-huh."

"Bent!" She stamped her foot with impatience. "Don't you hear what I'm saying?"

"You liked boys at twelve."

"You were twenty-six then," she reminded him.

"Too old for you, then, too."

"Not for an impressionable, rodeo-loving girl with stars in her eyes. You were young and gorgeous and fit and reckless. You were my hero, Benton Murray. *I was in love with you.*"

He was already shaking his head. "A twelve-year-old? Honey—"

"Don't 'honey' me, Bent. Don't try to diminish my young dreams. They were important to me then. Watching you helped form my own fantasy of winning the World. Watching you changed my life. And now you're my trainer. It's a dream come true."

She stared earnestly into his eyes, and he stared back, striving to understand her meaning, when at last he did. "Are you telling me that you still find me irresistible?"

She shifted her feet and dropped her gaze to the center of his chest. "Sort of."

A slow, welling satisfaction began deep inside and burst forth full and wide. He felt like a fool, standing under the tree and grinning like a rookie cowboy who'd just won his first buckle.

With the pad of his thumb, he nudged back his hat and relaxed. Her uncomfortable "sort of" had to be the most incredible, most arousing declaration of affection he'd ever received. And in his heyday, he'd received plenty.

"Well, darlin'," he drawled, "looks like we got no problem."

"What do you mean?"

"You want me. I want you. No problem."

Before he'd finished speaking, she was shaking her head. "You've missed my point. Nothing's going to happen between us, Bent. You believe I'm too young for you, remember? You're moving to Montana, remember? I'm sticking with rodeo, or some form of it, for life. You hate it, *remember?*" Her voice was rising, and her eyes went a little wild. "Nothing's right between us, Bent. Nothing can come of our sleeping together."

He didn't like her conclusion, but he didn't know how to argue the point. Control of the conversation was quickly slipping away, and with it, a measure of his satisfaction.

"I—I should never have given in to myself tonight," she concluded. "It's my fault and I take full responsibility. You're behaving like a typical man, trying to get what you can."

"Hey—I don't deserve that." His tone was quiet, reproving.

"Maybe. You *have* been trying to seduce me for months now."

"Only you, Kate. Not anybody else."

"Uh-huh." Her voice held clear notes of disbelief. "How do I know what you're doing, and to whom, when I'm not around?"

He ground his teeth together. "Because I've just told you so."

She half turned away, showing him her tense profile. "It doesn't matter. There's no commitment between us. You aren't beholden to me, nor I to you. We're just trainer and client. Teacher and student. We have a business deal that we're both upholding. Let's leave it at that." She started to walk away when he caught her arm.

"There's more than a business deal, and you know it. It won't go away just because you say so, Kate. There's a name for what you've got. It's called denial."

"I deny nothing. I simply refuse to take part in any more . . . physical encounters between us. Let me go."

For a tense moment their gazes locked and held, until finally he released his hold. "I'll be seeing you, Kate. Soon. Then we'll see." At a distance he followed her back to the house. When he was certain she was safely inside, he climbed into his truck.

Could Kate turn off her attraction to him simply because she decreed it? Could she ignore the building tension between them? He shook his head. If so, she was a hell of a lot stronger than he.

With the pickup door gaping open, he sat there a moment and stared at the deserted porch. The house looked dark, forbidding, and slowly the old loneliness wound its bitter tentacles around his soul. For a time, while he'd held Kate in his arms, the emptiness had retreated to the dark corners. Now that she was gone, it returned, its grip more painful than ever.

The next morning Kate left at dawn, all set to "go hard" on the circuit and garner each and every point she could. Trying not to think about Bent and their session beneath the oak was an exercise in futility. Each time she recalled his thrilling touch, she agonized over her weakness for him. She didn't like her loss of control.

Gripping the steering wheel on the long drive headed for Nampa, Idaho, for the Smoke River Stampede, she vowed never to let such a situation happen again. Rodeo was her love and her life, and some variation of it probably always would be. As she'd reminded him, Bent hated rodeos and resented the small bit of time he had to spend at them. He planned to bury himself on a Montana ranch. She could never live that way.

She sighed. She *could* fall in love with him. In fact, making a hard examination of her feelings, she admit-

ted she might already be half in love with him. It
couldn't be wise. Loving Bent would present a tremendous risk. She was less sure than ever that he was
capable of returning any woman's affection.

August passed, and then September was a crazy
month. The circuit went from Ellensburg, Washing-
ton, to Walla Walla, to Fort Madison, Iowa, back to
California for San Jose, and off again to the New
Mexico State Fair. Kate drove and rode and drove some
more. Flash helped and occasionally others shared the
ride.

By the end of the month, Kate found herself high in
some of the series standings and number fourteen in the
World standings. Being number one now was not required, but she must continue to maintain a position in
the top fifteen to qualify for Finals. At that time, all
standings would be thrown out and the fifteen final-
ists would be on equal footing.

At home, Mimi scoured the newspapers and watched
the cable television channels featuring rodeo, carefully
monitoring Kate's progress. For the new up-and-
coming star, Kate Monahan, there was a gradually de-
veloping media coverage.

The attention gratified Kate—with occasional print
interviews featuring quotes from her, or short television interviews asking her opinions on various riders
and horses and on her own ascending career. It meant
they were watching her, beginning to believe she had a
shot at the title.

Her life became a whirlwind of long drives, fast rides
and a growing monitoring audience. They called her

"Killer Kate" for her aggressive riding style and way of lying low on Sierra's neck, her blond hair mingling with Sierra's flying mane.

But the constant pounding put tremendous strain on Sierra's imperfect feet. The mare needed much care and Kate worried about her. For Sierra's sake, she was forced to telephone Bent and ask him to meet with her in closer intervals.

He agreed to meet her at the Kern County Fair Rodeo, in Bakersfield, where he lived. There he refitted the mare's shoes to keep her sound for a few more weeks.

Kate watched, and seeing Bent again made it difficult to concentrate on anything. He wore a black shirt, the sleeves rolled to his elbows, which revealed his vein-laced arms and sinewy muscles. His tanned face was solemn, his gaze watchful. "Hand me that nail I dropped, will you, Kate?" he asked, with Sierra's forefoot gripped as usual between his knees.

"Sure." She stooped, collected the nail and held it to him on her open hand. When he took it, his fingers brushed her sensitive palm. Memories of their embrace and her abandoned response to his touch came flooding back. A terrible yearning to press her face to his chest and draw in his familiar, comfortable scent forced her to swallow hard. She could hardly meet his eyes for fear he would see her hunger.

Bent held the nail Kate handed him tight in his fist. The cold iron was warmer from her touch. The thought of how warm *he'd* been with her body nestled against his squeezed in his chest. He studied the high color of Kate's cheekbones and guessed she was remembering their kisses. Good. He'd found it impossible to forget. Although he recognized that Sierra was in need of closer attention, he had to wonder if that was the sole reason Kate had called him. Perhaps, just a little, she'd wanted to see him?

Right now, it was obvious she couldn't even hold his gaze, so great was her self-consciousness. While he found it endearing for about five minutes, after that, her attitude began to eat away at him. Damn it, had he pushed her too far?

Without realizing it, he began mentally casting about, searching for ways to make her smile, to bring the joy back into her face.

Sooner than he'd expected, an idea surfaced.

Inside of an hour he was seeking out Flash Johnson.

"Did you hear, Kate?" Flash rushed up to her, bursting with news. "Bent's going to team rope with me in a jackpot here Friday. It's not a sanctioned event," he explained, "because Bent doesn't have his permit paid up, but a lot of the guys are staying after the rodeo to rope. Isn't that great?"

"Really?" Kate asked, hardly daring to believe it. "Bent agreed to this?"

"Yep. His idea." Proudly, he stuck out his thin chest.

"This is incredible." She smiled at Flash's happiness. What could have convinced Bent to ask Flash? Why would he have changed his mind?

Not that it mattered. She was thrilled. Tying Sierra at the shower rack to wait patiently for her daily bath, Kate rushed to Bent's truck and found him alone. He was eating a tuna sandwich and sitting on the top high step of his trailer, legs outstretched.

"Is it true, Bent? You've really decided to rope with Flash?"

He shrugged. "It's just a jackpot this weekend. After the rodeo."

"That's great." She was hard put not to throw herself into his arms. "I know you'll do fine. You guys are a great team."

"You're happy about this, huh?" He grinned, watching her closely.

"Well, sure. It means a lot to Flash. And I think you'll like it, maybe despite yourself." She lifted one brow, daring him to deny it.

He took another bite of his sandwich, chewing thoughtfully. "Maybe I will." He held out his sandwich. "Tuna?"

"Love it." She stepped forward, realizing too late that she would have to step between his outstretched legs. All at once her nerves jangled a warning. Hadn't she promised herself to keep her distance?

Already committed, she took a healthy bite and went to step back. He caught her arm. "Wait. Let me." Gently, he wiped at the corner of her mouth, where a crumb of bread clung. In his slow, lazy way, he smiled into her eyes.

From every part of her body, blood rushed warmth to her breasts and pelvis. She caught her breath and swallowed convulsively. The dry bread formed a hard ball in her throat and she choked. With a hearty hand, he pounded her on the back, then began a circular rubbing motion across her shoulder blades. How many nights had she lain awake, dreaming of his hands caressing her back, her arms, her breasts?

Spying a cola can beside him, she snatched it up and took a long pull. At last the bread went down. "Thanks," she said weakly.

"You bet." His I-want-to-touch-you smile was still firmly in place. "You'll watch, won't you?"

She stared at him, watery-eyed. "Huh?"

"When we rope. You'll stick around to watch?"

"Wouldn't miss it. I don't have to be anywhere over the weekend."

He formed that slow smile again, further confusing her. He almost acted as if her presence was very important to him. His eyes crinkled at the corners in a way she liked, and his grin was white and wide. "That's good, Miz Monahan. Real good. More tuna?"

Kate watched, all right, and she shouted and cheered Bent and Flash until she was hoarse. An exhibition of skill and speed, the team roping always thrilled her, and seeing Bent accomplish the exercise so well gave her goose bumps.

During the entire day, they took turns with some fifty other teams. Bent wore a concentrated frown, quietly encouraging Flash, and ignored the other ropers—even the sarcastic Barry Engan.

They did not win, but got a respectable third. "Flash, old son," Bent drawled as they dismounted at the end of the competition, "someday you'll get inducted into the Cowboy Hall of Fame."

Flash grinned broadly and Kate noticed he still hadn't let go of his coiled rope, as if unable to bear putting the precious thing down. This had been his best performance all year. "If I ever am, I'll owe it all to you, man. You're the best!"

Bent guffawed, denying it, but Kate could see his euphoria. He kept patting Ty Banning's buckskin, which he'd again ridden, and kept rubbing its lathered neck. Wisely she refrained from pointing out that his suppressed love for rodeo was the reason for his high. She *knew* his love for the sport hadn't died.

They led their mounts back to Flash's double trailer. Flash had used the eye-catching paint he'd always ridden for calf roping, and the gelding was proving even more adept at this event. As they unsaddled, Kate helped carry the bulky saddle blankets into the tiny tack room on the trailer and gave the horses only a small amount of water so they wouldn't develop colic. The men rehashed their several go-rounds and she listened, feeling satisfied with the day until Bent made a casual announcement.

"That was lots of fun, Flash, and you'll do even better when you get a real partner."

Kate whirled and Flash froze. "You don't want to rope with me anymore?"

"Oh, you need someone better than me. This was a one-time-only experience. I'm not gonna take up rodeoing again. I did all that, years ago. Nope, after this year, I'll be heading up to Montana." He stretched his back, oblivious to Kate's shock and Flash's profound disappointment.

Falling silent, Flash finished caring for his horse and loaded it into the trailer. "Gotta say goodbye to a few friends," he murmured, striding toward the thinning crowd.

Kate struggled with her own disappointment and watched Bent easily heft his heavy saddle onto a rack inside the tack room. After putting hay into the feeder bins, he loaded the buckskin. She noticed he was whistling, and she wondered at that. He wasn't the sort to go around happily *whistling*.

On a sudden intuition, she frowned. He sounded relieved. *Was* he relieved he wouldn't have to compete again?

She put herself squarely in his path as he went to close the back gates. "You're terribly afraid of failure, aren't you, Bent?"

He stopped. "What?"

"You're afraid that you'll come in last, be a disappointment, that you'll *lose.*"

He hesitated and his jaw flexed. "I roped, Kate. You saw it. I competed. And I didn't come in last."

Sadly, she shook her head. "Your glass shouldn't be half empty, Bent. Let it be half full. Sometimes you *will* fail, you know. We all do."

"I lost plenty when I rode bulls and broncs," he growled. "You're telling me nothing new."

"You have to disregard the possibility of loss and think *win,*" she urged, ignoring his protest. Always, he seemed to listen best when she was touching him, and needing his attention now, she didn't hesitate to reach out and knead his shoulder.

Instantly he went still. His next words surprised her. "I figured if I roped with Flash, it would put the sparkle back in your eyes. It seemed like something you wanted me to do."

She blinked. "You did it for me? But—but," she sputtered, "it's for *you* I want you to do it. It's to give you something fun in your life, Bent. You're too serious. I don't mean you should make a career of roping. But it's something to strive for—to learn and enjoy competing. To rodeo—"

"*Rodeo.*" He said the word flatly, warningly, and Kate knew exactly what he meant by it. How often had he said he wouldn't return to the sport?

They were off the subject. If she could keep him interested enough in the roping, the rest would take care of itself. "I wonder if you remember how to win, Bent. Is it possible you've temporarily forgotten—that you're thinking more of not losing, instead of going for it?"

Though he frowned, it appeared he was listening. She recalled his telling her about the year he'd failed to retain his title, and at the same time, failed to keep his wife. Could it be the two were so intertwined in his mind he couldn't separate them? "Even if you don't make it, your marriage isn't on the line anymore. You won't lose your wife, too, Bent."

A stain of color appeared beneath his dark tan. "You go too far, damn it," he exploded, and her heart sank, knowing she'd backed him into a corner.

"I'm sorry, Bent. I'm sorry. It's just that someone's got to tell you these things. Someone's got to—"

"That right? Who voted you into the role? I don't want your opinion about it, Kate. I've never asked for it." He bent toward her close and threateningly, his voice low. "Leave off with the pop psychology. I don't need it. If you don't, you might find yourself minus a trainer."

A tremor passed through her at his words. Yes, she'd been preachy, but he didn't mean it. Not Benton Murray. Not her hero. Going very still, she could hardly breathe. Her throat closed and she knew it would hurt, but she had to ask. "You'd quit me, too, Bent?"

Chapter Eight

"**I**'m no quitter," Bent snapped.

She said nothing at all. Still, he knew the pushy little thing would harp and nag forever if he didn't push back. Suddenly he had to get away.

At that moment Flash came back to take the trailer and Bent stomped off to his own truck, leaving a silent Kate to gaze after him, a ridiculously mournful expression tightening her features. What did she care, he wondered, gunning his engine to life, if he ever swung a loop again? What stake did she have in it? None, that's what. She was interfering and bossy.

He drove around Bakersfield angrily, going nowhere in particular. The woman had a lot of nerve—calling *him* a quitter. He'd never quit anything in his life. He'd merely retired.

After a while, he stopped for a burger and fries and ate them in the truck. He had originally planned to stay at the arena grounds and keep Kate and maybe Flash company for the evening.

As furious as he was, he made a new decision to head home. Tomorrow he'd have to go back for a shoeing job he'd picked up. That was soon enough to endure Kate's accusations.

Pulling up to his three-acre Bakersfield ranch, he entered the small cabin-style home and threw the truck keys onto a dusty table. The house had only two bedrooms, it was cold, not particularly clean, and never cheerful. Dishes from breakfast were still on the table and the dirty clothes hamper was full. The bed wasn't made, either.

No wonder, what with chasing Kate all over the country these past months and spending so little time at home. Disliking the mess but in too dark a mood to clean it, he kicked an old boot into a cobwebby corner, slammed shut a gaping drawer, then swore loudly when it caught his thumb.

Going to the tiny kitchen, he got out filters and threw spoonfuls of ground coffee beans into the maker, then stared at it while it bubbled and steamed. *A quitter.* She had no right. No right at all.

When the coffee was done, he poured a mug, hot and strong and black, then pushed aside the soiled dishes to sit at the table. Planting his elbows on the wooden top, he took a gulp of the hot brew, hardly caring when it burned his tongue. Before his mind's eye came visions of Kate: Kate careering around the barrels, Kate yelling at him, laughing at him, Kate's face softened in moonlight as he stroked her. There was a lot to like about her, he conceded to himself. She was feisty, yes, but around her a man was never bored. And she was seldom wrong about people or her observations about life.

But she was wrong about him.

Wasn't she?

A vague unrest propelled him to his feet. Taking along his mug, he walked outside and went to the small barn and corrals where he kept Sarah's old gelding and two gentle saddle horses. A sassy, strutting hen pecked around the yard, looking for a rooster to lord it over, Bent figured sourly. The old gelding came to the rail to snuffle his hand, his wise, patient eyes asking ancient questions.

For no reason at all, memories of his short marriage to Alicia flooded him. Again he relived his year of fame, riding the crest of the wave, performing better and ever better until it all culminated in fabulous triumph. Beautiful, sophisticated Alicia had been at his side for every rodeo. She'd loved his winning, loved to be beside him when he won money and trophy buckles. She'd worn his buckles with pride, and he'd liked her wearing them.

Until it all came crashing down the following year when he'd finished outside the top fifteen—ignominiously not even qualifying for National Finals. It seemed only a month or two later when Alicia had announced, somewhat aloofly, that she was leaving him for Tex Kilburn, whose baby she was, incidentally, carrying. At least, she thought it was Tex's. Maybe it was Bent's. She didn't know, didn't particularly care.

Tex had also, perhaps *incidentally,* won All-Around World Champion Cowboy that year. Bent had seen photos of Alicia's beautiful, proud face right beside Tex's in *ProRodeo Sports News* when he supplanted Bent as the next big star.

The humiliation had been equal only to the pain.

Coffee cold now, Bent tossed the dregs onto the ground and grimaced at his morose thoughts. It was all so long ago. Within a year Alicia had given birth to Sarah and been killed in that airplane crash with Tex. Bent was out of love with her by then, but he didn't think he'd ever get over the bitterness—nor would he forget his lesson about women.

But he had quit rodeo for good.

He'd quit.

For the first time he considered whether what Kate kept saying might have some minute bit of truth. *It's for you I want you to rope,* she'd said. *To give you something fun in your life.*

Was he a quitter, giving up on rodeo, on women, almost on life itself all these years since his wife abandoned him? Had he been blaming her defection for his lost rodeo career?

Absently, Bent scratched the gelding between the ears and thought of his pleasure when roping with Flash. So much of the old joy had resurfaced—the heat of competition, the surging horseflesh beneath him, the earthy smells of dust and effort, the triumph of a job well done.

Kate had somehow made it her business to urge him to take up the gauntlet again, compete against his peers, but in an entirely new event. Could he put his pride on the line to do it?

No answer was forthcoming.

Long after darkness fell over his small ranch, Bent wrestled with his thoughts and, turning in, was no closer to a conclusion.

In the morning he showered, dressed, stamped his feet into boots and drove back to the rodeo grounds.

Kate's truck was gone, and after experiencing a moment's loss, he guessed she had left early for the next rodeo.

He shrugged to himself. What would he say to her anyway?

The cowboy who wanted two of his horses shod waved and said he'd lead them over. Bent nodded, setting out tools and readying his truck for work.

"Saw you ropin'."

Bent turned sharply at the taunting drawl. Barry Engan leaned one hip on the hood of Bent's truck, a cigarette hanging negligently from the side of his mouth.

"Did you?" Bent resumed his work, choosing the iron shoes he thought might fit the small quarter horses being led over.

"Came in third, didn't you? After my first." Engan rolled his cigarette around in his jaws.

The remark stuck like a sliver beneath his skin, but Bent did his best to ignore it. There was nothing to say to the jerk.

Engan, apparently not getting the rise he wanted out of Bent, spat out his smoke and ground it out with his boot. "See you around." He turned away, then made an obviously carefully executed turn back. "Oh, a little advice. Maybe you'd best stick to horseshoein'. You do that real good, anyway."

Hot anger flared. Though he'd been able to ignore the other man until now, in Bent's heart the old rivalry was instantly revived. Years back, he and Engan had gone head-to-head all year riding roughstock, their winnings nearly equal. At National Finals they'd also been equal—until Engan had a bad fall. Bent never did know if he was the better man.

Since the roping yesterday, Bent had been more than happy with his third-place finish. It was a great showing, considering how little of it he'd done in recent years. But now he wanted first—over Engan—or nothing.

About to issue a challenge, as he and Engan had done to each other years back, he belatedly recalled that he'd told Flash and Kate he would not compete again. Words of challenge withered in his throat as he stared after the swaggering Engan.

Choking with frustration, he watched the other man saunter off, his cigarette still trailing a dying bit of smoke on the ground beside the truck.

"'Killer Kate again rounds the barrels on flying hooves of triumph,'" Mimi read to Kate over the telephone, where Kate was getting ready to compete in Temecula, California. "The article goes on to talk about your mare, 'The Bay Bomber.'" Mimi chuckled. "I like that name for Sierra."

Kate smiled. "Yeah. It suits her." She drew a deep breath. "Well, I'm doing pretty good, Mimi. Top fifteen. If I can keep it up here and through the Grand National, we'll be headed for Vegas. What do you say?"

"I say point me to the slots."

Laughing, Kate agreed. Already it was October, with San Francisco's Grand National looming with its big prize money beckoning like a beacon. Saying goodbye to Mimi, she hung up the pay phone and headed back to her trailer, as she'd done so many times before.

Naturally Bent would join her for the Grand National, and it was crucial that Kate do well there. She hadn't seen him lately and, damn it, she missed him.

Missed his sly sense of humor, his sardonic grin, even his contrary ways.

The man had burrowed under her skin, become an integral part of her life. Even though she didn't see him every day, she thought of him. Mostly she thought of his kiss and the hard strength of his arms encircling her. A quiver went through her at the memory. Many nights as she lay in her trailer bed, she'd imagined him holding her, whispering words of praise and affection. It helped her get to sleep on lonely nights.

Days later she came in at the top at Temecula. After that, it was straight up the coast to San Francisco's Cow Palace. She was exhausted from the long haul, but upbeat.

Parking her truck and trailer alongside others, she got out and went around back immediately to see how Sierra had fared the long trip. The rodeo was already under way, but since she had drawn up for the second day's performance, she didn't have to ride tonight. However, Flash was calf roping, and she wanted to watch him. Unloading Sierra and walking her around to stretch her legs, Kate stabled her where she was shown and made sure the mare had feed and water before wandering to the chutes.

Saying hello to friends and acquaintances, she hadn't long to wait. Beneath bright arena lights, Flash shot out of the box after the calf, his paint gelding a streak of black and white. He made a good catch on the calf, but instead of smoothly sliding off his horse, his toe caught in the stirrup and he fell, ignominiously, to the ground.

He got up and scrambled to tie the calf, but the precious seconds could not be made up. As he remounted and rode back, a few of the guys chuckled, and his mortification was obvious in the red flags of color flying on his cheeks. Kate bit her lip and wondered what to say to him.

Before she could get close to him, she saw Bent striding over to put his hand on Flash's shoulder. Kate paused. She'd been unaware that Bent had already arrived. Seeing him for the first time since their confrontation when she'd accused him of quitting made her steps falter. Hopefully he wasn't still angry with her; as mad as she'd seen him get over the past months, he didn't appear the type to carry a grudge.

Slowly she approached them. Flash was speaking vehemently.

"I'm gonna do better, Bent. I can, I know it."

"Course you can, Flash. And you will. Don't let those yahoos get to you." He indicated the bunch of grinning cowboys waiting for their turns to rope.

"Jackasses," Flash muttered.

"Nah," Bent surprised Kate by saying. "They're a solid bunch of guys. And they like you. You just gotta learn to laugh at yourself, that's all. Everybody does stupid things sometimes."

"Even you, Bent?"

He laughed. "Yeah. Even me." Catching sight of Kate, he turned toward her, eyes wary, and tipped his hat. "Kate."

"You made it," she said unnecessarily.

"Did you think I wouldn't?"

She lifted her shoulder. "I . . . didn't know."

"I won't quit you, Kate," he said lightly, but she read a wealth of meaning behind his words.

Suddenly a tremendous weight lifted from her heart. "I'm glad. I need you."

To cover the rush of emotion engulfing her, she turned to Flash. "I'm sorry about your fall. Bad luck. The catch was a thing of beauty, though. If you hadn't hooked your toe, you'd have won."

Flash blinked twice, then brightened. "That's true. I had that calf in about four seconds."

Still muttering, he led his paint away, leaving Bent and Kate to face each other. For a moment they simply looked into each other's eyes, and Kate felt the rodeo, the people, the noises and the animals fade away. There was no one else in the world but her and Bent.

"You ready to ride tomorrow?" he asked quietly.

"Right as rain." Digging her hands into her front pockets, she began to feel shy. "If I do well here, we're going to Finals."

"I know."

She bit her lip, getting shyer still, but determined to ask him something. "If I win, will you go to dinner with me? To celebrate? I'm buying."

A slow smile began forming, relaxing his hard mouth, and as he drew his gaze leisurely down her body, he sighed in pleasure. "Honey, I don't need food when I'm around you. I could just swallow you whole."

"Bent," she said warningly. But she didn't really mind. Not at all.

"All right. Guess I could force down a thick steak."

"Nope. We're going to the House of Prime Rib, and we're having all the trimmings. Baked potatoes dripping with butter, fresh asparagus spears, sourdough bread baked on the wharf—"

He whistled. "You're making me hungry. That does it, I've made up my mind. I want that prime rib dinner. You'll just have to win."

Laughing, Kate enjoyed his teasing. She saluted him. "Yes, sir. I'll go tell Sierra right now."

With Bent watching from the chutes the following night, Kate came in first. On each successive night she managed to perform well, and after her last run she didn't have to look at the timer to see that she was, indeed, going to Vegas. She could read it in Bent's face.

Leaping off Sierra, she flung her arms around the mare's neck, then around Flash, around the laughing stock contractor, grizzled and gray-haired Randolf Raddin, and finally, around Bent, who swept her high in the air. He whooped and she laughed, reveling in the emotional high.

I'm going to National Finals, she sang inside. It had to be the happiest day of her life. Her goal of security for Mimi was closer than ever. "Want that dinner now?" she asked Bent.

His grin was wide and white. "All the trimmings?"

"Everything." She laughed again simply for sheer joy, and when others came up, she accepted their hearty congratulations. Still breathing hard from the exertion of the run, she was interviewed by a sports cable network, and tried to be poised and articulate, giving credit to her great horse and especially to Benton Murray, "the best farrier and trainer on the planet."

The following night she and Bent got to their celebratory dinner. The House of Prime Rib featured warm, low lighting and rich, velvet wallpaper, linen tablecloths and heavenly smells of fabulous food. Bent ushered her inside, and Kate liked the feel of his hand at her lower back. He wore a black suit with bolo tie, his cleaned-up gray hat and shined black boots. Cheeks sleek from a fresh shave, Bent cut a dashing, handsome figure, and Kate found herself unexpectedly awed.

As they waited to be seated, he teased her about her interview. "Best trainer on the planet," he mimicked. "Weren't you overdoing it a little?"

"No, I didn't 'overdo it,'" she returned. Smoothing her white, sheer-sleeved coatdress, she hoped she looked pretty enough to deserve the handsome man. They were seated and served a good Sonoma County Chardonnay. She took a sip and studied him over the rim of her glass. "You are the best. I should have said in the universe. Next time I will."

Bent tasted his own wine thoughtfully. "You've earned the right to go to Finals, Kate, as one of the top fifteen barrel racers in the world. I said you were good. You proved it."

The waiter appeared and they both ordered. Feeling incredibly warm inside, she wasn't yet ready to give up the subject. "You always had unshakable faith in me. It...helped me to win, Bent, knowing you *believed* I could. I'm so happy I found you."

She shouldn't have put her thoughts into words; she knew it when his eyes grew hot and possessive. But she felt like hugging the world tonight, and Bent was such a big reason for her success, she couldn't keep it contained.

"Six weeks, Kate, till Finals." He reached across the table and took her hand. "You'll be able to rest, and rest Sierra. Then you can train some, keep in shape. Then, after Finals..." He hesitated and she hoped he wouldn't mention that thing about going to bed with him.

He frowned as if knowing it wouldn't be right saying it—not tonight.

Besides, if he did figure out she was just as wild for him, age difference or no, there would be no fending him off.

Every time she thought about his moving to Montana, she got upset. Between his hard work shoeing horses and his training percentage from her winnings, she knew the money he'd earned had put him very close to his goal. Soon he'd be able to afford that ranch.

"So, do you plan to buy your Montana property in the near future?" she asked, unable to stand wondering any longer.

"No rush," he replied easily. "I've been thinking about it for ten years now. A few months either way won't matter."

"Oh." She guessed a noncommittal answer was better than a flat statement that he would desert her. Their dinner served, she set aside her wineglass and took a small bite of beef. It was tender and delicious.

After Finals, technically she wouldn't need him anymore—not in a trainer sense. Win or lose, this season had been exhausting; she couldn't even think about going hard again in January. In any case, there would be nothing to keep Bent around, no reason for her to see him or Sarah anymore. She had learned enough to continue.

Bent tucked into his meal enthusiastically, then insisted on paying for the dinner. They had a small tussle over the bill, which Bent won by virtue of his bigger muscles. Kate smiled when he wrestled the bill away and accused him of being too macho to let a woman buy his dinner. He surprised her by admitting it.

As they left the restaurant and drove away, Kate fell
silent. She opened the window and breathed in the
briny sea scent of San Francisco's coastal wind, letting it brush coolly across her cheeks.

"What's wrong?" Bent asked, maneuvering his
truck down Van Ness. "You're too quiet."

"Nothing," she forced herself to say. "Everything
is just perfect." She smiled to make him believe it, but
inside she knew a dismay that alarmed her. Her euphoria over winning was shadowed by the specter of
Bent's Montana move.

Sooner or later he'd pack up and go, and she would
be alone.

Thanksgiving Thursday it rained all day, but Bent
and Kate sat close together on Mimi's couch after a
sumptuous early dinner. It had been a long five weeks
since the Grand National and Kate was well rested. She
worked Sierra just enough to keep them both in shape.
She'd bought lengths of scarlet and white satin and
sewed herself a beautiful shirt to wear at Finals. Mimi
had added fringe at the yoke. It hung now, pressed and
ready, in Kate's closet.

Tess and Sarah had arrived that morning, as had
Flash, to help prepare and eat to their heart's content.

While everyone else was sprawled in various stages
of overstuffed contentment, Flash pressed his nose
against the wet window and lamented, "Why doesn't
it stop raining? I can't practice roping during this
downpour."

"Take a break, Flash," Bent suggested. "Have some
more pumpkin pie."

"Oh, no," Mimi interjected quickly. "He's already
had four pieces. I need some for my breakfast."

"*Breakfast,*" Bent exclaimed good-naturedly. "Don't tell me you're gonna eat pie in the morning?"

"Do it every year, don't I, Kate?" Mimi said.

"She does," Kate confirmed, liking the feel of Bent's large frame pressed lightly along her side. "After every Thanksgiving, Mimi sneaks out of bed early, goes into the kitchen and gets the leftovers. She has the entire dinner over again—even down to the gravy on the mashed potatoes."

"And pie," Flash said glumly. "I can't have any more because she wants it for breakfast. Every year it's the same. I'm starving and all I hear is 'Don't eat the pie, Flash.'"

Everyone laughed except Flash, and Kate knew a wonderful happiness infuse her. The heat of the fire crackled cozily against the backdrop of spattering rain on the window. Combined with the warmth of Bent's thigh alongside hers and the presence of her family, she was filled with peace and a sense of well-being.

She would enjoy this day with Bent. It could well be one of her last. The poignancy made her heart ache.

She might not win the World at Vegas, but she would still be a finalist—an honor in itself. She *would* win, however, with the support of her family and the encouragement of Bent.

"Help me with this, Dad," Sarah asked Bent from where she sat at a card table. She was fitting together a thousand-piece jigsaw puzzle of a red-painted barn and brilliant fall colors of turning maple leaves.

"Sure." He got up and Kate decided to go into the kitchen for a mug of hot coffee. Flash was already there, begging Mimi for a half slice of pie, and she grinned as he was adamantly refused.

"Now, I'm making a basket for you to take home to your ma, Flash, including a piece of pie, and I expect it to get there." Mimi hesitated. "I sure wish she'd come over some year. When I think of her all alone in your house every holiday—"

"She doesn't want to come, Mimi," Flash told her quietly, and Kate frowned, knowing his mother was probably at some bar, drinking with her cronies.

"I'm going to check on the barn," Kate told the two, suddenly remembering the leak in the roof that might be dripping on Sierra.

"I'll come," Flash offered, forgetting the pie.

Together they ran out the back door, through the rain, holding newspapers over their heads. Once inside the barn, comforting horsey smells of warm hide and hay and leather greeted them, along with the mare's welcoming nudge. The leak was not bad and nowhere near the horse, so Kate took up her newspaper again, prepared to dash back to the house.

Flash touched her arm. "I'm real proud of you, Kate, going to National Finals, and stuff."

She hesitated, lowering the newspaper. It was the first time he'd said so since San Francisco. "Why, thank you, Flash. That's nice."

He studied his boot tops. "I didn't do so well this year. I don't guess I'll be able to 'go hard' again. In fact, I've been thinking of getting a job somewhere hereabouts in Riverside."

"Yes, that's right." Frowning, she recalled their conversation months ago about this. Because he had made no money this year on the circuit, he'd used his savings, and that, apparently, was nearly gone. At eighteen years old, Flash had to think of his future.

"I need to help out my ma," he said, adding to her thoughts. Though the woman hadn't been much of a mother to him, he still felt a deep obligation to her, and this Kate grudgingly admired.

"You need a trade, something someone will train you to do," she said, thinking aloud.

"But what? Trade school takes money." He stared at her as if she ought to know the answer, and oddly, she, too, felt as if she should. Though only six years younger than Kate, Flash somehow made her feel worlds older. She'd often thought of him as the baby brother she'd never had. She felt responsible for him.

"You could go around town, maybe check in at the feed barn, see if you could get a job there. Ask at the local riding stable. They always need people to muck out stalls and do general maintenance."

"Sure," he agreed weakly, and Kate felt her heart sink. Her ideas were stopgap at best. Flash needed the stability of a career, or, as she'd suggested, a trade. He deserved better than raking manure, and he was capable of so much more. They both knew it.

Her frown deepened and she tried not to show her worry about him. She *must* come up with a solution to this problem. After all, Flash was family.

Together they walked back to the house, the rain tapping on the newspapers they held aloft.

The hours passed pleasantly into afternoon, then early evening, when everyone decided that although they weren't exactly hungry, they *could* stuff down a snack. With a mischievous, youthful grin Mimi produced two extra pies she'd been saving, much to Flash's delight.

The rain let up and Bent rose reluctantly from Kate's side by the blazing fire to drive Tess and Sarah home.

Flash helped Tess carry out a few of her dishes, and Sarah took a plateful of leftovers. Bent kissed Mimi's lined cheek, then lowered his head to kiss Kate's mouth right in front of everyone.

With a wicked grin, he set his hat jauntily on his head while Kate touched her lips with her fingers. "See ya next week," he called.

"Yes. Next week. In Vegas." She raised a goodbye hand and stood on the porch with Mimi for several minutes after they'd all left, staring sightlessly out into the gray mist. "Mimi, do you think I can do it?"

"You'll do it, honey. You'll win because you love to race, because Sierra does just as much. You'll win because you're the best barrel racer ever."

Doubts filled her. "I don't know, Mimi." All year she had eagerly looked forward to the most famous rodeo of all. She wanted it, wanted the competition. But on the eve of possible victory, now she was more frightened than she'd ever been. So much could go wrong, so many variables. Then where would Mimi be? Her money gone, spent on sending Kate "down the road," and with no championship title to show for it.

Sure, she had made good money this year. But a big part of it had gone to travel expenses and some would have to be used to pay off her expensive truck and trailer.

And who was she, Kate Monahan, to think she could win the most coveted prize of them all?

A touch on her arm surprised her. Mimi urged her into a wicker chair, then sat next to her. Looking deep into Kate's eyes, Mimi spoke quietly, compellingly.

"If you don't win, Kate, if you knock down every single barrel, fall off like Flash did, it's okay. Listen carefully, honey—I give you permission to lose. Don't worry about the money, we'll get along fine. Don't worry about a thing. You understand? I believe you will win. But if you don't, the world won't come to an end." She stroked Kate's cheek, and Kate felt her lips trembling.

Suddenly she threw herself into her grandmother's arms and wept—all her pent-up doubts and hopes pouring forth in a storm of release. Always, this wonderful woman had been there for Kate. Always, she'd been a rock of calm stability. "Thank you, Mimi," Kate whispered, throat raw. "I'll do my best."

Mimi patted her back. "Of course you will, sweetie. That's all I've ever asked of you."

The steady strength of maternal love enclosed Kate like a shield against the world. She wiped her eyes, stronger already. How wonderful to have Mimi's support and love.

Her back stiffened and she drew in a deep breath, then gave the older woman a watery, confident smile. "The hell with 'my best.' I'm gonna win, Mimi. You just watch me."

Chapter Nine

The glamour, the glitter, the awe-inspiring lights of Las Vegas, Nevada, all made Kate go wide-eyed and full of wonder. In the encroaching darkness of evening, enormous lighted signs of flamingos, cowboy boots and palm trees flashed and strobed in a wild kaleidoscope of color. Nothing she had seen across the western states compared, and Kate was completely dazzled.

As she drove Mimi slowly toward the Thomas and Mack Center, making a side tour through the city streets, Kate craned out the window so much that Mimi chided her, "Stop rubbernecking and watch the road."

"Sorry," she mumbled. "But look at that huge Spanish galleon in front of that hotel."

"Forget the boat," Mimi exclaimed, herself forgetting about watching the road. "Check out the volcano at that one!"

After oohing and ahhing all the way down the strip, they turned off onto Paradise Road, headed for the center. There they unloaded Sierra and then went to check into the hotel where many of the competitors were staying. Ten performances were to be held on ten consecutive nights, and Kate had been keyed up all week.

At the hotel, Kate left Mimi perched on a stool, cheerfully feeding quarters into a slot machine. Feeling restless, she went back to the center. She found Bent lifting her mare's front hoof inside the stall. Her heart lifted. It had been a week since she'd seen him Thanksgiving Thursday; it felt like a year. For long seconds she simply allowed herself to drink in the sight of him. Boots, jeans, hat—he was pure, handsome, heartbreaking cowboy.

She sighed and leaned on the stall door. "How's Sierra look?"

When he straightened, something reflected light at his midsection. "She looks good," he replied. "Let's keep her legs wrapped, just in—"

"You're wearing a buckle," Kate gasped, staring at his belt. "Is it…?" Coming closer, she peered close to read the engraved writing. "National Finals Rodeo All-Around Champion, Benton Murray." She sighed. "You're actually wearing your trophy buckle. I can't believe it."

He lifted one shoulder. "It seemed important to you."

The admission pleased her out of all proportion. Did this mean he was going to stop denying his rodeo legacy? Whatever else she might guess, he *was* wearing it for her. She smiled into his eyes. "I would imagine you'd be proud of it. If I win the World, I'm wearing my buckle every day. Even at night when I sleep."

He laughed. "What about when you take a shower?"

"Then, too."

"I'd like to see that—your belt and buckle slung around your hips and you naked—wearing nothing else. Or maybe your hat, too. You could wear that."

"Hush." She fought a blush at the ridiculous picture he'd created. Sierra extended her nose to blow gently in her face, and she reached out to stroke the mare's soft nuzzle. "Oh, Bent, I'm so excited to be here. I've never been to Vegas."

"Neither have I. When I rode, Finals were held in Oklahoma City. They didn't move here until '84. From what I've seen so far, though, it's a hell of a town."

She hugged herself. "Sure is. I can't wait to see it all. The casinos, the shows—"

"*You* won't be seeing much of it," he corrected. "Early to bed, early to rise, good food, light training, that's your life for the next ten days."

"But I want to play blackjack. At home I always win against Mimi and Flash. I've got a method I'm sure will beat the house if I could just—"

"Forget it. As your trainer, I'm pulling rank." He gave her a mock glower, then glanced at his watch. "Since your first performance is tomorrow night, you'd best get some sleep. I'll stick around here a while longer, keep an eye on Sierra. Get along now." Leaning over, he surprised her by dropping a quick hard kiss on her mouth.

He shooed her out and reluctantly she left, knowing he was right. Yet she felt the imprint on her lips for hours as she readied for bed. Trying to sleep, she thought of the sold-out crowds who would be watching her tomorrow, of the expectation and speculation about who would win. In the dark hours tossing on her lonely hotel bed, her father's negative words echoed in her head. *You don't have what it takes.*

It wasn't possible to erase his edict. Still, she'd made it this far. She'd made it to Vegas. Would he have been proud of her? She'd never know. But she could put whatever closure on the situation she chose. Had he lived, perhaps, eventually, he would have beamed approval at her from the stands.

Knowledge of Mimi's faith and even Flash's unflagging support took some of the burn out of the harsh memory. Girding her most of all was Bent's profound belief in her talent. His confidence kept her buoyed during the too-quiet hours of the night. Maybe, just maybe, the balance hung within herself. No matter what, she was determined to be captain of her own destiny. Thinking of Bent's steady confidence, she could almost believe in victory.

She woke from a restless sleep, atingle with stress and excitement. After a quick room-service breakfast of yogurt and cereal, she dressed, then headed for the rodeo grounds. She felt edgy, nervous. Her face must have reflected her tension, because a waiting Bent showed her nothing but cool professionalism, for which she was grateful. Right then she didn't think she could deal with fending off sexual overtures.

"How're you feeling?" he asked, studying her closely.

"Nervous." She glanced around at nothing in particular. It was hard to concentrate on any one thing with the ten-day run looming before her. "Scared stiff, actually. Terrified."

"Okay, okay." Bent turned her away from him to massage the taut tendons in her neck. His strong fingers worked their magic and she sighed. "I won't tell you to relax. It's not possible and you need to be keyed up. So focus. Visualize yourself and your mare coming around each barrel perfectly. Imagine riding square in your saddle. Picture winning."

She closed her eyes as his hands slid down her arms to clasp across her stomach. Needing him, she leaned back and enjoyed the brief moment. "Yes, master," she intoned.

He chuckled in her ear, then kissed it. "You've still got a sense of humor, so all is not lost." He turned her back to face him. "You'll do fine. Come on, I'll give you a boost up."

He'd already wrapped Sierra's legs and saddled her. When he'd settled Kate in the saddle, he had her canter the mare in the practice area to warm up, giving her tips, reminding her of proper technique. Encouraging her. His very calmness amid the bustle and noise of people and animals and color lent Kate a strength she desperately needed.

Mentally and emotionally she clung to him, drew a measure of serenity from him. He was there for her; he always had been.

In the first two performances, she finished third and fourth, but made good enough time to keep up her average. The average was the combined times of all ten performances, and this would determine the world winner, so it was not imperative that Kate win each run. However, she could earn money winning individual performances, and so she tried to focus on this.

During the other events, Kate noted that Bent carefully watched the team ropers, Barry Engan in particular. One night, as he closely observed his former rival, Kate could see Bent's hard fist close around his rope. He'd taken to picking it up once in a while, she'd noticed. Guessing he simply wanted to get reacquainted with the feel of the twisted nylon-poly texture, she wisely made no comment.

"Watch this," Engan said to Bent from the box. "Maybe you'll learn something."

His partner, the heeler, chuckled and readied his loop. The calf was released and the riders careened after it, ropes whirling overhead.

When it was all over Engan's time proved close to the record. Engan rode by, coiling his rope and grinning, ear to ear, right in Bent's face.

Bent nodded once and said, "Not bad, Engan. Not bad," though Kate could tell it cost him. He'd probably hate her voicing the notion that he had a big heart—that he wouldn't begrudge even a man he disliked a word of praise. Bent was a good man, she realized. A wonderful man.

Even if he wouldn't admit it, she could see he wished he were competing.

It gave her hope.

At seventeen, Sierra was aging and troubled by uncertain hoof conditions. The mare would have been put to pasture by many another rider. But Kate learned nightly that never was there a mare born with more "try." Infirmities or no, she still ran hot and eager right through each performance, like an enthusiastic young filly. With Bent's careful monitoring, she kept in good shape.

By the fifth night, Kate began to win and earn money—over five thousand that first evening's win. Her average came up, and her times were within split seconds of another rider, comely Darita Tibbons. Darita was a great favorite with the media for her dark flashing eyes, buxom figure and flirtatious manner. Her striking, lightning-fast black gelding made Darita quite a spectacle.

If Kate kept up her times, she had a good chance at the average. During the day she slept in, ate well with Mimi, Flash, and often Bent, shopped at the Cowboy Christmas Show at Cashman Field and, as Bent decreed, retired early. The days were long because she lived for the nights.

"You're doing fine, Kate," Bent said, covering her hand with his own as she waited her turn for the seventh performance, perched tightly atop Sierra. Tonight she wore her crimson satin shirt and a cream-colored Stetson hat. Sierra's red leg wraps echoed the color in her shirt. The horse sidestepped, anxious to run, to fulfill her destiny. Bent took a step as the horse moved, keeping his hand warm and firm on Kate's. Beneath his hat his eyes were a glowing amber that exuded confidence in her ability.

"Keep it tight around the first barrel," he reminded her. "And no leaning. You're the best. You're the best." His low, litanous voice helped build her up, and she kept her gaze locked on his. He was so generous, this man, so giving of himself and his knowledge, and he gave to her freely. No one but her grandmother had ever cared what she did, if she won or lost or competed at all. Bent cared. Deeply. He had to, she just knew it.

And she cared for him. She loved him.

Time slowed and the rest of the world disappeared. Bent was the only man she'd ever wanted. From the time she was twelve years old hollering her lungs out for him, she'd been a little in love with him. Now, at this crazily critical time, her love threatened to engulf her in an avalanche of emotion.

"Bent," she whispered urgently. She inclined her head toward him, a sudden inescapable desire to tell him *now* rushing up her throat. "I—"

Blaring overhead, the rodeo announcer called her name.

"Come on, babe," Bent was saying. "Tonight's yours. You're the best."

She nodded. Later. She would tell him later, when there would be all the time she'd need. Business first. Swallowing back the words, she collected the reins tighter and bit her lip.

Still holding her gaze, Bent stood back. Horse and rider shot out. Kate hung on, *not* leaning, as they turned around barrels so sharply her stirrup nearly touched the ground. In the stretch Kate flattened on Sierra's back and urged the horse home. When they won again, Kate knew an unsettling combination of growing relief and mounting tension. Could they keep it up?

Right on through the last performance, Sierra ran her heart out for Kate, and on the final day, woman and rider bolted past the timer in a streak of crimson satin, glory and triumph. She had won the average.

Kate Monahan, World Barrel Racing Champion, took a victory lap with the winner of each of the other events and waved her hat high. The crowds cheered. Flash danced a replica of Kate's little jig, back when he and Bent had roped, bringing more laughter to the crowd. Mimi and Tess yelled, Sarah squealed and Bent simply grinned.

Kate wept.

But she cried happily, and mostly in Bent's arms. At the World Champions Awards Banquet on Sunday night, the rodeo commissioner pumped her hand and slapped her back and pumped her hand again.

"Killer Kate," the commissioner exclaimed, "you killed 'em all. Their times, anyway. Nobody could get close to you and that Bay Bomber. Congratulations."

"Thank you," she said humbly, unable to think of anything else. *Oh, daddy,* she thought inwardly. *I did it. I did have the stuff.* It was only then, holding her trophy buckle reverently in her hands, that she was able to forgive her father. He hadn't known the talent of Kate's horse, or the skill Kate would acquire after years riding her. Nor could he guess the incredible trainer his daughter would be able to hire. She liked to think that her father watched from Heaven . . . and was pleased.

Later that night, exhausted but contented, Kate returned to the near-empty rodeo grounds and went to give Sierra a piece of watermelon she had saved from the banquet. The place looked so different without the crowds. Yet it took little imagination to see it filled to bursting with noise and lights and confusion.

Flash was helping load roping steers onto a stock truck with the contractor and another calf roper. Sarah was there, watching, and seeing Kate, she came over.

"You were great," Sarah told Kate. "Some day . . . maybe I'll be like you."

"Thanks." Her reserves of energy drained by the long competition, she leaned a tired shoulder against the stall door. "Maybe we can convince your dad to let you barrel race."

"You think so?"

Kate nodded.

"I hope he'll let me. If I ever get to, will you help me sew a shirt like your red satin?"

Laughing, Kate assured her she would.

"Uh, can I ask you something?" When Kate nodded, Sarah plunged ahead. "Are you and my dad, uh, sort of together? You know, like a couple?"

It was an awkward question. "Sort of," she replied, hoping to evade giving a straight answer. "I'm not sure. We've been trainer and student for so long, but not anymore." She tapped her trophy buckle she'd proudly strapped on. "This changes things."

"I hope you will be," Sarah surprised her by saying. "My dad seems happiest around you."

Fresh hope surged in Kate's heart. "Does he?"

Sarah nodded solemnly. "You make him do stuff he says he doesn't want to. And he complains like an old bear. But then later, I can tell he's glad."

Tired as she was, Kate felt new life flow through her. She'd lost track of Bent more than an hour ago at the banquet. He'd been the center of attention among a group of old-timers swapping tales of crazy bucking bulls, wild horses and even wilder women. Most sounded too farfetched to be true, but the men swore by their authenticity.

Not for anything would she have disturbed Bent—not now when he seemed finally comfortable around his former acquaintances. And never had she seen him more ready to smile and laugh. Part of it was her success, and his as her trainer. But she knew that part of it came from his love of rodeo. She'd always known that love lived buried in his soul.

Morning would be soon enough to share her secret with him—her love. The truth was, now that she was out of the heat of battle, she wasn't quite so confident he'd take the information well. How would he react?

There were more interviews in the morning, and more people congratulating her. Offers came in immediately—Western clothing manufacturers, commentator jobs, young hopefuls wanting *her* to train them, sponsors. She was incredibly pleased, and promised to give the offers careful consideration. Now that she had reached her goal, she'd be able to care for Mimi without worry.

She had finished the year earning more than a hundred thousand dollars—enough to pay off her truck and trailer and all her travel expenses, replenishing Mimi's nest egg plus adding considerably more. At Finals, she had earned another twenty thousand. Money gave its own security, she mused. With her clothing endorsements and other deals, her income would skyrocket.

Because Mimi wasn't feeling well and Kate wasn't quite ready to leave, Flash offered to take Mimi home with him. Kate fussed over Mimi until the older woman waved her away, insisting she was fine, just needed to get back home and rest in her *own* bed.

At Flash's truck, as they were ready to pull out, Bent stopped him with an upraised hand. "Flash, old son, a word with you?"

"For the finest barrel trainer on the planet? Anything," Flash teased.

Kate threatened him with a closed fist for mocking her Grand National interview. She gave Mimi a goodbye hug.

Bent grinned briefly, then grew serious. "My business has grown quite a bit, what with my regular cus-

tomers in Bakersfield and those I've picked up around
rodeos. It's time I took on some help—an apprentice.
You'd be doing me a big favor if you'd consider it."

Flash's teasing grin turned into an expression of
astonishment. "A farrier's apprentice?" he echoed.
"You mean it?"

Bent shrugged. "If you're interested."

Flash beamed. "Am I! When do you need me to
start?"

"We'll talk." He smiled and tipped his hat to Mimi.
"Have a good drive, and you get some rest now,
hear?"

Backing away from the truck, Bent signaled Flash to
drive off. As he did, Mimi waved.

Kate could not take her eyes off Bent. She was afraid
to speak for fear of breaking down. By offering Flash
this job, he would be giving the young man a wonderful opportunity—something for which Flash would not
need extra schooling. Thereafter, Flash would be able
to earn a steady living in a valuable trade, one that appeared to fascinate him. And he could not get a better
teacher.

Heart filling, Kate wished she had the nerve to wrap
her arms around Bent's neck and give him a kiss he'd
never forget. She loved him. It was time to tell him.

She was about to do so when Darita Tibbons sauntered up.

"Mr. Murray?" Darita asked sweetly. "We met
briefly before. You remember?"

Kate didn't like the big smile Bent gave the curva-
ceous brunette. Nor did she appreciate the way he
nudged back his hat to look his fill. "I do, indeed."

"Well, I've discussed it with my father, and we feel
that I could use a good trainer—to improve, you un-

derstand. Would you be interested in the job? Daddy would pay you well—we know you've had loads of offers lately—and I told Daddy that we just had to get you before somebody else did."

"Interesting" was all Bent said, and Kate felt her temper begin to simmer. She'd never been fond of Darita, and now she knew a true dislike of the girl. What had she meant by Bent receiving "loads of offers"?

"Will you think on it?" she asked.

He continued to smile. "Sure will, Miz Tibbons."

The girl walked away. Was it Kate's imagination that the girl's tightly jeaned hips were swaying? She firmed her lips and demanded, "You've received other offers?".

"A few."

Hearing her shrewish tone, Kate tried to lighten it. "Well, that's, uh, wonderful. You could start a whole new career by training barrel racers." While she had expected to get offers, she hadn't anticipated him fielding them from other women, and never from her contemporaries. The idea of him in the same proximity with other females made her distinctly jealous.

"I don't know if I want to train anymore," he relieved her by saying. "It's a big commitment. A big hassle."

She frowned. Had she been such a weight to carry? Guiltily, she thought of the times she'd needed his encouragement. Nowhere in their verbal agreement had she said emotional hand-holding was part of the job description. It had .simply happened, and she was grateful. She had leaned on him. Maybe he didn't like that.

Her tone held a defensive edge when she said, "Sorry I was such a hassle."

"That's all right." His patronizing tone prodded her. "Anyway, I've got other plans."

"Yes, of course." She stiffened. "Your Montana ranch."

"Yeah. But that Darita..." He swung his head toward the direction in which the woman had sauntered off. "She is some package. Tempting. Mighty tempting."

"Her—or her offer?" Kate asked, feeling more mulish than ever.

He chuckled. "Just teasing, Kate. Making sure you still love me."

He said the words lightly—like a joke. But an instant tension gripped her. If only he knew what was in her heart.

"It's over, Kate," he said huskily. "Now, you'll come home with me."

Her eyes flew to his face. She knew what he meant. Was this to be the moment of truth?

The long year of putting him off was at an end. Though he hadn't made advances on her at all during the past ten frenetic days, she knew his patience was at an end. "I—I never promised to go home with you," she whispered.

"Yes, you did." He settled one fist on his hip. "Not in words. But in the way you kissed me back, let me touch you. In the way you're forever touching me. And I want you—always have."

"But—" She grabbed at the one thing that had stopped him before. "What about the age thing?"

He gave her a hard look. "I'll get over it. Now grab your stuff and let's load Sierra. You can follow me to

Bakersfield. It's a long drive and I want to get back before dark.''

The casual way he assumed she would sleep with him—repay him with her body for his services—made her head reel. She had had all year to consider how she would handle this very situation. Now that it was at hand, she was completely lost.

She was aware of only one overriding emotion, which threatened to choke her. Fear. Although she was in love with Bent, she very much feared he was *not* with her. He'd never stopped telling her that he *wanted* her, but that, she knew, was different.

Had she given her love to a man bent solely on seduction?

As much as a simple look from him made her heart pound, as much as his touch made her long for something more private and intimate, she knew in her deepest soul that she couldn't sleep with a man she loved but didn't love her. Loving him so, it would shatter her heart beyond all repair.

A sheen of cool perspiration formed on her upper lip. She shivered. Loving someone, she discovered, entailed taking the greatest risk of all. She'd thought herself brave. She'd thought she was daring.

Now she knew what she was. A coward.

In an agony of doubt, Kate tried to stall.

Bent watched the uneasy denial cross Kate's pretty features, and cursed inwardly. He knew an overwhelming need to at least get her commitment to him—to know the confidence that she was his, and only his.

But she balked.

Was it to be as he'd long feared? Now that his usefulness to her was over, would she abandon him, forget him?

Would she do as Alicia—drop him when something better came along? He was aware of the media frenzy over her, of all the businesses reps vying for her endorsement. To a young, heretofore unknown woman like Kate, the sudden attention would very likely go to her head.

How well he remembered the fame, the flashing bulbs of a hundred photojournalists, the heady adoration of thousands of fans. Everyone had wanted to be his friend. Beautiful women had followed him to his hotel room with the merest crook of his finger.

No! From deep inside, the cry of loneliness that had so long haunted him returned to wail, the sound echoing in his head like a mocking laugh. "Damn it, Kate," he grounded, feeling her slipping away even as they stood there. "I've waited a long time for you."

"You don't really want me, Bent. It's just the challenge of wooing and winning a woman that makes you say that."

"What?" he barked, amazed she could think him so shallow. "Any woman will do, is that what you think?"

She turned away and he grabbed her arm, yanking her to face him. She cried out and stumbled backward against the horse. It shied sideways in the stall.

"Don't," she said in a small voice, sounding like a little girl, and Bent knew a level of frustration he'd never before experienced. At his sides his fists clenched. He'd long accused her of being too young, yet he'd learned Kate was a grown, responsible woman. She cared about her family and friends, made efforts to see them happy. She'd even made him recognize a few home truths. No selfish child went to the lengths she did to insure such things.

Yet he didn't know how to tell her of his admiration. How did a man express what grew tender and fragile in his heart?

Unlatching the door, she opened it and stepped out. He followed, but dared not touch her. "Kate!"

He hated how she avoided his eyes. "Bent," she whispered, the sound of panic vibrating in her voice, "I...can't."

Quickly she turned on her heel and jumped into her truck. Before he could think, she had driven away, leaving him standing alone in the dirt. Alone...again.

Chapter Ten

Back at home in Riverside with Mimi, Kate went through the motions of taking care of business. She answered dozens of telephone calls from friends, acquaintances, and Western clothing reps. She hired a financial consultant, and he and Mimi helped her scrutinize two boot makers, then decided on the one with the highest quality merchandise. The company wanted cute, young Killer Kate Monahan to front their high-end models. With her fresh young looks, small, fit body and infectious smile, they'd sell a million pair, they said. Everyone would want to buy their boots. She sincerely hoped so.

She agreed to pose for a famous jeans manufacturer offering lucrative inducements. Journalists telephoned for print interviews. A company contacted her wanting to tape a how-to barrel race video and sell it through mail-order and saddlery stores to "share her secrets with the masses."

Three or four of the calls were cash-on-the-barrel offers for Sierra, and the amount of money they were willing to pay astounded her. Naturally, she declined, but it gave her a new idea—perhaps she might begin breeding the mare and sell the foals for a hefty profit.

Her days were filled, just as she imagined they would be, with meetings and decisions. Mimi couldn't have been more pleased, knowing this was what Kate had worked so hard to achieve. She screened calls and lent sound advice on business deals. She even helped Kate make the decision to rodeo the following year—but only in a few of the bigger events—for the sponsors' sakes, to keep her name before the public. Kate also considered investing in another fast horse or two and beginning to train them.

Through all the craziness, one thing ate away at her: she had to live with the agonizing memory of Bent's face in Vegas as she'd driven away from him. Knowing she had *not* reneged on any deal, she nevertheless felt she had. In the dark of each night, a confusing mantle of shame descended on her and she questioned herself over and over.

Did he care about her at all?

In the weeks since Finals, he hadn't telephoned. He hadn't written. He hadn't dropped by.

She supposed she had no right expecting him, or hoping for such things—not with the way she had simply walked out of his life.

On the other hand, what else could she have done? Followed him to Bakersfield and slept with him—given herself in payment? In her deepest, most intimate self, she had long wanted to make love with him; always, she had imagined a beautiful sharing of bodies and minds and hearts.

Not a cold sale.

The horror of the idea always made her feel exonerated—if only for an hour or two. Then, niggling whispers of her betrayal returned to haunt her. Also haunting her was the feeling that something might have been worked out between them, if only she'd had the courage to try. Perhaps they might have started dating—seen each other without the student/teacher labels she'd deliberately kept between them. Now those labels were more like barriers than protection.

At night she tossed restlessly, paced the house long after Mimi had fallen asleep, and wandered the field where she and Bent had shared such wonderful, passionate kisses.

Sometimes in the privacy of her room, door closed and radio turned loud, she cried. She missed Bent. Missed his grin, his voice, the hot, intoxicating gleam that came into his eyes when he looked at her.

"Whatever's the matter with you?" Mimi finally asked some two weeks after National Finals while Kate sat at a living room desk. Spread before her were legal documents and contracts and letters that needed attention. Instead of working, she kept staring out the window, mind blank.

"Wrong, Mimi?" Kate blinked, brought back to earth with a thud. She'd had such trouble concentrating since Vegas.

"You act so..." The older woman waved her hands as if helpless to find the right words. "So...lost. You traveled and rode all year, won the World, yet you don't seem as thrilled as I imagined you'd be." The older woman perched on the edge of the couch and laid a dishtowel in her lap. "Isn't this what you want, honey?"

After a hesitation, Kate said, "Yes. Sure. Of course it is." She picked up a pen and peered at a contract but saw nothing. Mimi sighed and Kate again lifted her gaze to stare out the window.

Mimi was right to question her, Kate thought, wondering at herself. Wasn't this what she'd wanted? Why hadn't it fulfilled her? Why, now that her dream had come true, did she find no joy?

Laying down her pen, Kate tried to smile at her grandmother, but managed only a weak twisting of her lips. Giving up, she rose and quietly let herself out the screen door to walk to the barn. There, she haltered Sierra and led her to the arena, turned her loose and watched while the mare raced in circles, stretching her legs, then rolled in the weeds.

From the house came sounds of Mimi's old sedan starting up, and absently Kate remembered that Mimi had mentioned going to the grocery store after eggs and milk.

Kate leaned on the railing, watching Sierra. She might as well admit it to herself—she was merely going through the motions. Instead of looking forward to each new day, she found herself ever more miserable. She was no longer happy with the World title. In her mind, the title and Bent had become intertwined. Again, Bent's proud, angry face as she'd left him materialized in her mind.

For the first time she let herself recall everything about their last conversation. Replaying it slowly, she at last recognized what she'd missed, what she had subconsciously ignored. In Bent's expression there had been frustration, yes. And a kind of impotent rage. But there was something else. Something in her confusion she hadn't noticed—or perhaps she simply hadn't wanted to see.

Pain. Pleading. A vulnerability she hadn't thought Bent capable of. Hadn't she learned he was a man who carefully guarded his heart, protected his emotions? Hadn't he revealed so much of himself that she instinctively knew he was sharing it with her alone?

From such a private man, his confidences were a kind of gift—a trust she hadn't fully recognized at the time. Now, in the fullness of reflection, she did. Bent had given much of himself.

And she had given him so little.

In the corner of her eye she saw Flash amble up the driveway toward her, his dear, friendly grin in place. "Howdy," he said. "How's every little thing?"

"Fine," she replied dully, unable to summon a smile. "I'm glad to see you."

He scratched his head. "Coulda fooled me."

She did try to smile then. "Sorry. I'm not in the best mood today. Maybe I'm tired."

"Maybe you're sad."

She picked at a thumbnail. "Why would I be sad? Everything's going great—just like I planned, like I always wanted."

Invariably polite, Flash removed his fraying straw hat and studied the leather band. "You sure? Seems like we shoulda seen Bent around here by now. You two have a spat?" With one eye, he squinted at her through the sunshine.

Emotion abruptly rose up to lodge in her throat. *Damn.* When had she become so transparent? Unable to speak, she kept her eyes on Sierra, now grazing. She would not cry. She would not cry. She would *not*.

"I don't know what went on between you two," Flash said carefully. "None of my business. 'Course I'm young and don't know much. But I've learned one thing and it's this. If you don't have what you want, try for it. If you fail, try again. Don't sit around pining after it."

He was right. Of course he was. Kate glanced at him, and his understanding, compassionate expression almost did her in. She held back a sob.

"Oh, Flash." She gripped the rails with both hands and forced herself to breathe normally. "I miss Bent so much."

He shrugged his thin shoulders. "Then go get him, girl."

She chuckled, a watery, halfhearted sound. "You make it sound simple."

"Isn't it?"

"I don't think so." She hesitated. "What if he's, uh, lost interest?"

The way he lifted a brow reminded her suddenly of Bent. "Could happen, I s'pose," he drawled. Then he grinned, big and wide. "But I wouldn't bet on it."

Kate summoned a smile. Laying a hand on his arm, she cleared her throat. "Flash, have I ever thanked you for being my friend?"

"Sure," he said without pause. "In all kinds of ways."

She nodded. Overhead, the winter sun shone clear and diamond-bright on the pipe rails, and the roof of the house, and on Flash's reddish hair.

It was as if the fog had cleared and everything she'd worried about was explained. Answers to murky problems stood out in sharp clarity. She knew what to do.

Saying no more, she started for the house, gradually increasing her pace until she was at a trot. The trot turned into a lope, and by the time she got to the back door, a gallop. Now that she'd decided her course, there was no time to waste. Suddenly she had the panicky sensation of time draining from an hourglass, of a life-or-death horse race, of a ticking bomb about to go off.

Inside the empty house, she raced to her bedroom, hauled out her old suitcase and stuffed in jeans, tops and her toiletry case. Flash followed, standing in the kitchen doorway. When she came in to tape a note to the fridge for Mimi, he said, "Hey, where's the fire?"

In a mad rush, she grabbed her worn sheepskin coat and cream-colored Stetson hat off the rack, got her purse and keys and ran down the front steps. "Next year," she called over her shoulder, "I want you to enter some of the rodeos with me. We'll only go to a few of the biggest. I'll stake you."

The youth halted in his tracks. "What?"

Tossing everything inside the truck, she cranked the engine to life and jammed the transmission into reverse, tires crunching gravel. Out the open window, she yelled, "Oh, I know you're going to work for Bent soon, but you'll get some time off. You'll be a champion roper someday, and I want a piece of the action. Keep practicing, 'cause now you've got a sponsor."

"Wow." A beatific smile spread over his face as he reached her truck window. "You sure you can, uh, afford it?"

She smiled back, thinking of the boot deal alone, then all the conservative, long-term investments she had planned. She and Mimi would be comfortable for years to come. "I think I can swing it," she answered.

"But no slacking off. I expect lots of practice from you." Of course she knew no one would or could work harder than Flash.

"Yes, ma'am," he said smartly. "Uh, where're you going?"

Her smile faded. What if her plan failed? What if Bent wanted nothing to do with her, rejected her, hated her?

"To Bent's," she answered softly.

"Thought so," Flash said, a superior grin forming on his angular face. "It's about time you stopped mooning around after him and did something."

Kate stared straight ahead. "I haven't been mooning."

He rolled his eyes. "Yes, Miss Sponsor, ma'am."

Though Kate had never been to his Bakersfield home, she knew his address and didn't think she'd have trouble finding it. The long drive gave her time to think about what to say.

What if he wasn't home? What if he was so angry he wanted nothing more to do with her?

She'd wait for him. She'd keep trying until they reached some sort of agreement. No matter what, she wouldn't give up. Each time a doubt surfaced, she gritted her teeth and forcibly squashed it.

Heading down a country road on the outskirts of town, she spied a battered mailbox with numbers that matched his address, and, behind that, a long driveway. Taking a deep, deep breath, Kate turned the truck onto the rock-lined drive. Her fingers trembled on the steering wheel. The house was a small log cabin, and not far off, a pole corral housed two sleepy-looking geldings. The bit of grass lawn was badly in need of a mow, and a mower sat out front as if somebody had intended to get to it, but hadn't.

Bent's work truck was parked at a lazy angle to the house, as if the driver hadn't cared much where he'd left it. Kate coasted to a stop and chewed on her lip. He was here.

As she got out of her truck, her legs shook. Her nervous laugh sounded out of place. How silly. She was here for a straightforward proposition: to find Bent and somehow make up with him. To tell him she needed him in her life.

Maybe even to tell him she loved him.

Her boots crunched on the rock drive as she made her way instinctively toward the small barn instead of the house. When she neared the double doors, she heard the familiar, reassuring clanking of hammer meeting anvil, then the whine of the grinder. The noise had probably masked her engine, or, like many country dwellers, he would have come out to see who'd driven up. It was crazy, nonsensical, but the comforting sounds of Bent's work brought an ache of longing to her throat.

In the doorway of the well-lit barn, she paused and found him tending a horse. He saw her at the same moment. He stopped short, with a horseshoe gripped in one gloved hand, and his eyes narrowed dangerously.

Twined fingers trembling, Kate lifted her chin and prepared to speak. Instead of words, she found she could utter nothing beyond his name. Her throat had closed up.

For long frozen seconds, Bent stared at her. "What do you want?"

She took a step forward and swallowed convulsively. Because of her nerves, her voice came out raspy and low. "Bent—I need to get some things straightened out. I...need—"

"Why'd you walk away from me at Vegas?" he demanded in surly tones. He looked rumpled, his hair uncombed beneath his hat and several day's growth of unshaven beard on his cheeks.

"I didn't want to—"

"You think you can *use* me and light out, just like that?"

"I—I was afraid," she replied haltingly, "of getting used myself."

Instead of the annoyed answer she expected, he tossed the iron shoe onto a workbench with a bang. He fixed his gaze on the far wall, as if unable to bear looking at her.

Her spirits sank. Had she driven him so far away?

"The hell you say," he rasped, his jaw flexed. "You kept me around for as long as you needed a trainer and farrier. After you won the title, it was 'See you later, cowboy.' You dumped me." He turned to pin her with amber eyes as hard as jewels.

"Bent, there's a reason for that," she said, pleading in her voice. She raised a hand toward him beseechingly. He looked at it as if she were offering him a dead rat. He was so angry, so bitter, she wondered if everything they'd shared would be lost. If she were responsible for driving him deeper into the solitary despair and aloofness that had kept him alone all these years, she would never forgive herself.

Gathering all her strength, she had to force the words out. "I couldn't sleep with you because...it would have broken my heart."

He snorted and, with jerky movements, stripped off his leather work gloves. "Great."

"I couldn't let you use me." She pushed on past his sarcasm. "Couldn't let you use me for one night, then watch you walk away." For a timeless heartbeat, the air between them was still and silent. Kate felt light-headed, like one does before a faint. But she'd never fainted in her life. The trembling had reached her knees now. With great effort, she hung on to her composure, her sanity.

Suddenly Kate decided to throw caution to the winds. She had nothing more to lose. Nothing. "Maybe if I didn't love you," she whispered, "it would be easier."

Shock formed on Bent's taut features. He stiffened as if shot and stared into her eyes, unblinking. At his sides his work gloves dangled, forgotten.

He's angry, she thought, hope draining out of her like air from a spent balloon. *He never bargained on this. Never wanted my love.*

Her shoulders slumped. "I'm sorry, Bent," she said from a throat raw with emotion. Inside her chest a vise squeezed. She wouldn't take the words back, wouldn't even if it were possible, because nothing she could say would change reality. She did love him—even if he didn't return her feelings.

Suddenly she felt as if her knees were giving out, and she glanced around a little wildly for a hay bale or chair on which to sit. There was none. Putting out a hand, she leaned her weight on the heavy sliding barn door and closed her eyes. In a minute she would leave—drive out of his life. But right then she had no strength, no will to move.

Eyes wearily shut, she heard a stall door open and the clip-clop of a horse being led into a stall. She opened her eyes.

Bent was headed toward her with the most determined expression she'd ever seen glittering in his eyes. Though she'd long trusted him, his surprising intensity gave her a moment's fright. He'd never been predictable. Never been completely safe.

A split second later he'd swept her into his arms, holding her high against his chest. She cried out, startled, but he walked out of the barn toward the cabin in long strides. His boots crunched with the sound of purpose on the rock drive.

She clung to his neck. "What are you doing?"

He didn't answer, and when he entered the house and kicked the door shut with his boot heel, she couldn't guess his intentions. Inside it was gloomy, save for a swath of sunlight coming through an open window. She had the brief impression of cluttered clothing and a few dishes, and then of a short hallway leading to two bedrooms.

For an instant she wondered if he would take her to his bed.

Yet he backed up to the blue plaid sofa and, where the sunlight came through, sat down, settling her onto his lap. Before she could think, he gathered her up and took her mouth in a very thorough kiss.

Kate stilled. He hadn't thrown her off his property. He hadn't ordered her away. He was kissing her like a man too long without what he needed. Like a man denied a craving and then abruptly getting what he wanted.

Her.

He wanted her—she could feel it in the crushing grip in which he held her. Could sense it in the desperation she tasted in his kiss, could smell it in the very scent of his skin. Kate moaned. Bent's need and passion for her were like the most addicting drug—the most intoxicating brew—the most compelling elixir she'd ever imagined. Behind his neck she laced her fingers together and yearned to hold on forever.

After several very satisfying minutes, he lifted his head and smiled at her tenderly. His voice was gruff. "You thought I was headed for the bedroom, didn't you? Honey, I wasn't going to push you into anything."

"You weren't?" Despite her great relief, Kate was still shaking, yet managed to arch disbelieving brows. "You've been telling me all year you were taking me to bed."

He shifted his weight on the sofa and grinned ruefully. "Well, in the beginning, I admit I, uh, considered it."

"*Considered?*"

Gently he reached up to run his forefinger down her cheek. "All right. I was going to do it. But when I got to know you, to respect your tenacity and bravery, well, I guess that was when I fell in love with you. And I decided I could wait. I just wanted some kind of sign that you cared, that's all."

Eyes big as teacups, Kate heard only one phrase. She couldn't believe it—couldn't quite take in the words.

Or could she? "You're in love with me?"

He shrugged a big shoulder, and she reveled in the emotion gleaming in his expressive eyes. Pulling her head onto his chest, he hugged her. She drew in a deep, grateful breath, loving the warm feel of his hard body. "I was about to come get you," he admitted. "Every day when I woke up, I told myself I was just gonna jump in the truck and drive to Riverside and grab you."

"Grab me?" She laughed, her heart feeling lighter than it had in weeks.

"Yeah. But... I didn't think you really wanted me. I kept remembering how you drove away. You made it look so easy. Like you didn't care one way or another if you ever saw me again."

"No, Bent," Kate rushed to assure him, loathe for any more misunderstandings between them. "I've been miserable without you." Placing her palms on either side of his tanned cheeks, she pulled his face down to hers and kissed him with every ounce of love she possessed.

When the kiss ended, he tucked her face into the crook of his neck and nuzzled her hair. "All I know is, I can't live without you. I need you near me even if you're giving me hell or pushing me somewhere I don't want to go."

She smiled tremulously and touched his mouth with her finger. "Like the rodeo?"

He sighed. "Yeah, like rodeo. I've learned things from you—even though I'm supposed to be older, wiser, more mature."

"What have you learned from me, Bent?" Kate asked in wonder.

He slid his callused palm beneath her braid to rest his hand on her nape. Collecting his thoughts, finally he said, "That it takes courage to try a task you're not sure about. It's hard to risk failure. And I've learned too well . . . that I've been a coward."

"A coward! You?"

"You made me look at the worst case scenario. What's the worst that can happen? That I'll fall flat on my face. But I can get up, like Flash did when he got dumped off his horse. I'll dust myself off and try again. And from you, I've remembered how to win."

"That's wonderful, Bent." She planted a kiss on his chin. "I didn't realize I was teaching you such things."

"You taught them by example, Kate." He shifted her off his lap to sit snug beside him in the filtering rays of friendly sunlight. Taking her hands, he looked deep into her eyes. "You made me realize I've been blaming rodeo for the failure of my marriage."

"Oh, Bent." She gazed at him with conflicting emotions: pleasure that he acknowledged it, sorrow that he'd had to go through such pain.

He frowned. "It's like you said. Rodeo gets in your blood and there's no escaping. I want to try and do better at team roping."

"You mean it? Hooray!" She couldn't help bouncing on the couch.

"Just to beat Engan, you understand," he said. But Kate merely smiled. She knew it was much more than that. She recognized in him the eagerness for competition. She could see that at least part of Bent had healed. His esteem had improved, and she was glad she had some responsibility for its rebuilding.

Then he shocked her all over again. "Guess we'll just get married. And don't say no because you'll have to get used to me."

"I will?" she said blankly, his proposal overwhelming her so much she could hardly think.

"Yep. I want you and Mimi to move to Montana. Flash will come, too. You can do anything you want there." He kissed her again, then looked at her hard. "No matter what, we're going to be together."

Kate listened with brimming eyes and a full heart. "You sound so sure, so positive everything will work out."

"Why not? If we love each other, the rest will come easy."

She picked at the buttons of his shirt. "Promise me one thing—you won't throw our age difference in my face if we argue or disagree."

He smiled. "I swear it."

Kate smiled, too. Benton Murray loved her, wanted her for his wife. The notion was awesome, thrilling. The man she'd always loved now loved her back with a depth of feeling that matched hers.

Gazing into into his intense eyes, she could never doubt it again. "With you, I'll have the home I've always wanted," she murmured, knowing a fulfillment in her heart that had been missing. "For myself, and for Mimi."

"Would you mind..." He hesitated, then went on, "if Sarah comes, and Tess?"

"I'm crazy about those two." She chided him for even voicing such thoughts. "Montana, huh? I've seen the mountains there. They're beautiful."

"And the streams and the lakes and wildlife and—"

"And rodeo?"

Reluctantly he shrugged. "I guess I'll never get away from rodeo."

"Nope," Kate replied succinctly. She slid back into his lap, where she'd longed to be for months, and kissed his neck. "And you'll never get away from me."

* * * * *

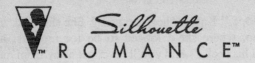

Silhouette
ROMANCE™

COMING NEXT MONTH

#1102 ALWAYS DADDY—Karen Rose Smith

Bundles of Joy—Make Believe Marriage

Jonathan Wescott thought money could buy anything. But lovely
Alicia Fallon, the adoptive mother of his newfound baby daughter,
couldn't be bought. And before he knew it, he was longing for the
right to love not only his little girl, but also her mother!

#1103 COLTRAIN'S PROPOSAL—Diana Palmer

Make Believe Marriage

Coltrain had made some mistakes in life, but loving Louise Blakely
wasn't one of them. So when Louise prepared to leave town, cajoling
her into a fake engagement to help his image *seemed* like a good idea.
But now Coltrain had to convince her that it wasn't his image he cared
for, but Louise herself!

#1104 GREEN CARD WIFE—Anne Peters

Make Believe Marriage—First Comes Marriage

Silka Katarina Olsen gladly agreed to a platonic marriage with
Ted Carstairs—it would allow her to work in the States and gain her
citizenship. But soon Silka found herself with unfamiliar feelings
for Ted that made their convenient arrangement very complicated!

#1105 ALMOST A HUSBAND—Carol Grace

Make Believe Marriage

Carrie Stephens was tired of big-city life with its big problems.
She wanted to escape it, and a hopeless passion for her partner,
Matt Graham. But when Matt posed as her fiancé for her new job,
Carrie doubted if distance would ever make her truly forget how
she loved him....

#1106 DREAM BRIDE—Terri Lindsey

Make Believe Marriage

Gloria Hamilton would only marry a man who cared for *her*, not just
her sophisticated ways. So when Luke Cahill trumpeted about his
qualifications for the perfect bride, Gloria decided to give Luke some
lessons of her own...in love!

#1107 THE GROOM MAKER—Lisa Kaye Laurel

Make Believe Marriage

Rae Browning had lots of dates—they just ended up marrying
someone else! So when sworn bachelor Trent Colton bet that she
couldn't turn him into a groom, Rae knew she had a sure deal. The
problem was, the only person she wanted Trent to marry was herself!

MILLION DOLLAR SWEEPSTAKES (III)

No purchase necessary. To enter, follow the directions published. Method of entry may vary. For eligibility, entries must be received no later than March 31, 1996. No liability is assumed for printing errors, lost, late or misdirected entries. Odds of winning are determined by the number of eligible entries distributed and received. Prizewinners will be determined no later than June 30, 1996.

Sweepstakes open to residents of the U.S. (except Puerto Rico), Canada, Europe and Taiwan who are 18 years of age or older. All applicable laws and regulations apply. Sweepstakes offer void wherever prohibited by law. Values of all prizes are in U.S. currency. This sweepstakes is presented by Torstar Corp., its subsidiaries and affiliates, in conjunction with book, merchandise and/or product offerings. For a copy of the Official Rules send a self-addressed, stamped envelope (WA residents need not affix return postage) to: MILLION DOLLAR SWEEPSTAKES (III) Rules, P.O. Box 4573, Blair, NE 68009, USA.

EXTRA BONUS PRIZE DRAWING

No purchase necessary. The Extra Bonus Prize will be awarded in a random drawing to be conducted no later than 5/30/96 from among all entries received. To qualify, entries must be received by 3/31/96 and comply with published directions. Drawing open to residents of the U.S. (except Puerto Rico), Canada, Europe and Taiwan who are 18 years of age or older. All applicable laws and regulations apply; offer void wherever prohibited by law. Odds of winning are dependent upon number of eligibile entries received. Prize is valued in U.S. currency. The offer is presented by Torstar Corp., its subsidiaries and affiliates in conjunction with book, merchandise and/or product offering. For a copy of the Official Rules governing this sweepstakes, send a self-addressed, stamped envelope (WA residents need not affix return postage) to: Extra Bonus Prize Drawing Rules, P.O. Box 4590, Blair, NE 68009, USA.

SWP-S895

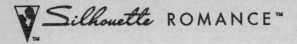

Silhouette ROMANCE™

Silhouette Romance presents the latest of Diana Palmer's
much-loved series

Long Tall Texans

COLTRAIN'S PROPOSAL
DIANA PALMER

Louise Blakely was about to leave town when Jebediah Coltrain made
a startling proposal—a fake engagement to save his reputation! But
soon Louise suspected that the handsome doctor had more on his mind
than his image. Could Jeb want Louise for life?

Coming in September from Silhouette Romance. Look for this
book in our "Make-Believe Marriage" promotion.

DPLTT

As a Privileged Woman,
you'll be entitled to all these *Free Benefits*. And *Free Gifts*, too.

To thank you for buying our books, we've designed an exclusive FREE program called *PAGES & PRIVILEGES™*. You can enroll with just one Proof of Purchase, and get the kind of luxuries that, until now, you could only read about.

BIG HOTEL DISCOUNTS

A privileged woman stays in the finest hotels. And so can you—at up to 60% off! Imagine standing in a hotel check-in line and watching as the guest in front of you pays $150 for the same room that's only costing you $60. Your *Pages & Privileges* discounts are good at Sheraton, Marriott, Best Western, Hyatt and thousands of other fine hotels all over the U.S., Canada and Europe.

FREE DISCOUNT TRAVEL SERVICE

A privileged woman is always jetting to romantic places. When <u>you</u> fly, just make one phone call for the lowest published airfare at time of booking—<u>or double the difference back</u>! PLUS—

you'll get a $25 voucher to use the first time you book a flight AND <u>5% cash back on every ticket you buy thereafter through the travel service</u>!

SR-PP4A

$\mathcal{F}$REE GIFTS!

A privileged woman is always getting wonderful gifts.
Luxuriate in rich fragrances that will stir your senses (and his). This gift-boxed assortment of fine perfumes includes three popular scents, each in a beautiful designer bottle. <u>Truly Lace</u>...This luxurious fragrance unveils your sensuous side. <u>L'Effleur</u>...discover the romance of the Victorian era with this soft floral. <u>Muguet des bois</u>...a single note floral of singular beauty.

YOURS FREE!

$50 VALUE

$\mathcal{F}$REE INSIDER TIPS LETTER

A privileged woman is always informed. And you'll be, too, with our free letter full of fascinating information and sneak previews of upcoming books.

$\mathcal{M}$ORE GREAT GIFTS & BENEFITS TO COME

A privileged woman always has a lot to look forward to. And so will you. You get all these wonderful FREE gifts and benefits now with only one purchase...and there are no additional purchases required. However, each additional retail purchase of Harlequin and Silhouette books brings you a step closer to even more great FREE benefits like half-price movie tickets... and even more FREE gifts.

L'Effleur...This basketful of romance lets you discover L'Effleur from head to toe, heart to home.

Truly Lace... A basket spun with the sensuous luxuries of Truly Lace, including Dusting Powder in a reusable satin and lace covered box.

$\mathcal{C}$omplete the $\mathcal{E}$nrollment $\mathcal{F}$orm in the front of this book and mail it with this Proof of Purchase.

PROOF OF PURCHASE

SR-PP4

Offer expires October 31, 1996